# MEN

# OF

# BLOOD

## *A novel by*

# BART LESSARD

DOCKYARD PRESS

For A.M.

# MEN OF BLOOD

Since the earliest of Moorish days it had stood atop a rocky inlet, rarely troubled, never touched, the village that would die. Fisherfolk called it home, and down generations the cots set above narrow tides had changed little, if at all—wash on daub, bright as teeth. Even the recent sweep, a third of Valencia driven out, had not undercut the population. Luck, perhaps—and fate, that a day so calm should see them vanish all at once. Calm but hot, fiercely so, noonday sun without a trace of cloud. The air clung like raw glass and a thirst for shade kept the people well indoors. All boats stayed on the slipways, lateens furled tight. Out on the sea blue met blue without hope of a rig. So none could expect anchors to drop, davits sway, hulls scrape aground. Yet here they were, landing craft, two dozen strong. A galley and its oars made do without the wind, as could this fleet of six. Ransom was not the aim but chattels, and any wretch between cane and crib was fit for sale. To flush them out thatch was set ablaze. The day went dim and hotter, the

3

sun a copperpiece behind the smoke. Whoever did not struggle to a quicker death was driven to the launches.

The raiders were a mix, just as many renegades out of the northwest as Amazigh moors. But they all wore the beard of the opposite coast, and the gown, and even the most ungodly of them took a name of faith. One born Jan now went by Suleyman. He led the raid and the whiskers set him off, red without a sunnah dye. His fellow turncoats, all Dutch, knew him yet by Jan. As he was rowed ashore, sleeve to brow, the catch knelt on the pebbly beach. Once aground he marked what was being said under that sob and rattle. Allahu la ilaha illa huwa, and so on. Moriscos. A redhead under the dey of Algiers knew a thing about making a show of piety. But the master in Salo would not be choosy. Too convincing in their Christianity—that would sell it.

"Where is Musa?" he asked. His favorite, proud but nowhere among the victors.

A crewman said, "Gone in. That woman, she broke a pot on his head and ran with her brat. He got a swipe in but wanted more." Smiles all around for those from the Netherlands. Long war in the provinces had left no love for Spain or for anything so arguably Spanish. A sword wound was a fine remark on forty years of strife.

The captain took no part. A tickle crept, and he dug into his beard to deliver a scratch. "You there"—to the nearest man, a mercenary in desert wrap. A gesture made it clear. The Tuareg bid a friend to come—scimitars ready, both men quick to Jan's heels.

* * *

Above the inlet was a headland, and the crest flew the wreck of a cart. Back when archers could be hired out, this had been hauled up for a target, and with no small pains. But times had changed and old arrowheads had been prized from the wood to be melted down for cleats and hooks. Weather had left a tilt, an axle thrown for good, and beneath that long slump was a green-eyed boy of nine. He wore a cordbound shirt of linen and he fought to keep a breath. For lack of sun the dirt was powdery and bare, and his fingers worried at the silt. A bullseye now a hiding spot, poor for the use. No less sure to draw attention was the body of a woman, not six feet before the spokes. Through at last with dying— fingers of her blood had sought a hold but the spread had quit. To the far side of the cart was a clutch of rock, then a drop.

The boy stared out. Past the boards sunlight was too bright to penetrate, and through that glare a noise came on: the scrape of cigales in the grass. Such a howl was nothing new but had grown mad to his ear, unearthly, a voice of fear and beating sun. Images came at a rush— people cut, burnt—and he was swept along. But a new sound brought him back. Clear even through the insect whine, steel had rung to steel.

He inched up to the spokes and looked to the victim, the bloodied shawl. Her face would have shown him features much like his own but it was turned away. Horror at the sight, but no recognition, whoever she had been. And beyond: a duel, hard fought. Two swords, two men. One of these was the village sentry, which meant the one man there who kept a sword. The other was Musa, and the hunt had not gone well. A dot had led him—blood in plenty—but on chance a vanguard party of his crew mates had stamped out the track. They had lost their own chase, too—women and children led out, what few the sentry could find—and without knowing it, on their return from nearby olive groves, they had spooked his up toward the cart.

Musa would never know as much. What he did, and too well—after some heckling from his friends, making quick back to the loot—was the anger of this brown infidel. The underbrush served him out once Musa was alone, and he found himself beaten back, back, up a slope. There any skill could find advantage, and Musa had never sold himself shy. On the foredeck, lunging with the captain's gift, he had tallied up the finesses. But no—it was all Musa could do to raise the pretty sword, thwart a stroke. His chin and knuckles ran with cuts, and a speckle was on his caftan. He cursed, he pleaded, but the Valencian man had no ear or heart to spare.

The fight grew near, and the boy shrank back. One man should have been familiar, but all was struck new. He had never imagined the spectacle, this bout to the death. Much like dance, he saw, unlike the slaughter downhill—dance, yes, even with a music underneath. No less a step to it, no less a tune and rhythm.

And at that thought—that truth—something dormant in him woke.

Harangues from the grass were shut out. The gleam of steel led his mind. Up he crept, mystified not by what he saw but by what he understood. Step, counter—he had the sum before it came. And just as rapt and fearless he saw a hand struck off.

Musa was less brave. A change of weight, no more at first, but sight of living marrow in living bone drew the shriek. Hand and weapon had lit near the cart. No chance for a knee, to marvel at the wound: the sentry had sprung. Backward Musa went, reeling—boots clipping stone—and the captain's favorite toppled without further noise. Even the splash below was lost.

No rest for the sentry—he stooped to the woman to touch the unseen face. To his came grief, in a hard wince. Standing up, he searched about left and right. "Joaquim!" he cried. A look to the cart gave nothing; shadow hid too well. His eye went back to the smoke. "Joaquim!" The slope led him down, weapon yet in hand.

All was still. The insects sang again. Joaquim—that had been his name. He had been staring at the treasure. To claim it he crept into the open. A blade was nothing new, but he had never seen one like this. Nor could any on that coast. A variety of shashka was what the boy now took up—the "long knife" favored by the Zaporozhian host. Fullered steel, more than a yard of it, with a slight curve, one edge, and no crosspiece save for a nub at the forefinger. Unlike the weapon of a Cossack this was made of crucible steel, from a wook ingot that had come farther yet. The metal had a turbid look but frozen, a seethe of ice, and bore a vine inlay. Ottoman and Cossack only met in war. Neither alone would account for the make. The origin was a mystery and chance had brought it far— duel on duel to that young hand.

The sentry had taken no blow, but there was a smirch on the blade. Joaquim took up the hem of his shirt. There his mother's blood, not yet dry, laid its final stain.

"Can a child go mad?"

Jan and his Tuaregs stared on. They had done so through the approach. Columns rose yet from the fires—sparsest shade, no relief. At the bottom of the slope Jan and the Tuaregs had left the guard to gasp like a stranded fish.

The swart boy had seemed to frolic from that distance, and he made no try to flee up close. In hand was a weapon. These were a swordsman's moves, uncanny—feint, lunge. The blade was as long as the boy was tall. Both hands were set to a hilt meant for a single grip.

"For all that silly flapping about," Jan said, "he almost looks practiced."

The Tuaregs looked to him for a word they could understand. He stared on. Thrust, guard, counterstroke, never with an eye to trouble just ten yards off. Jan considered the woman on the ground. Perhaps it was born of grief. Unfortunate—but then Jan noted the make of the sword.

"He has Musa's lascar weapon"—lascar for the dead seaman whose grip he himself had prized it from. Such cheek. A marketplace had uses for a saucy whelp. Jan puzzled out the Algerine words. "Take him alive," more or less. A firm hand in the cove would tell where Musa had gone.

Hefting weapons, the Tuaregs set to capture the boy. And still he had no mind for either, even as they chided him with a laugh. Nor did the maneuvers slow.

On a frown Jan turned to face the smoke. The thankless trudge had lent a good view of the lading underway— salted fish, sheaves of grain, the slaves, casks of wine and olives, whatever could go out.

All at once the day went bright. Jan looked up to skies grown clear. The wind was on the rise, and smoke from the raid dissolved above the sea. Surprising, and unseasonal, a westerly on that corridor of trade. Crown frigates would be on the prowl again, and those captains had less love for rescue than they did for a hull shot and a cold heap of moors. Get you to sea, Jan told himself.

Faint and innocent, no louder than a tut, the noise that came down through the summer whine. But his attention did roam upward, without concern, and what he saw left him to a gape. With a meaty grumble bowls were rolling to him, a pair of equal size. Face wraps came undone like bolts spread at market. Bare and astonished, those Tuareg faces that met his feet. Two heads lost—in a trice and a single stroke.

Jan looked to the boy, who stood between victims. Only one had fallen, and the other came down rigid but for the knees. The boy paid no mind to that topple—all his attention was now on Jan. In that small face green eyes were as bright as lamps. Daring a move—with a leer that the man born there would come to wear often.

The hush weighed down as the cicadas fell mute. Up came a gust of wind. The raveled strips went high, flew to the cliff, twisting in the drop.

"Enjoy your freedom," Jan said in Dutch, and he turned into the pelt of dust with a palm up before his eyes.

That last foe of three grew small and, once pride allowed it, fast. In victory the boy had but one thought. Never—he never need fear again. The backsword took a swab, and another stripe was drawn upon his shirt. Geniet van je vrijheid, the redbeard moor had said. Joaquim could only guess at what the words meant.

A question soon forgot. Nor did he find out—though had he in time for being caught, a smile would have met the answer. Laughs came quick to the man who took the name Vanderas, most often for a gloat. But there was no crowing now, twenty-seven years and nine hundred miles from that first glimpse, here in the mud, with manacles at foot and wrist. Head in a droop, he let the wet embankment prop him up. It was another kind of summer, one of Lancashire, a slow gray sop. His face was bruised and unshaven and his hair hung dripping from a red barretina. A clean diagonal lay across his shirt, the shape of the strap that had borne his arms. He shook at a chill and had no friend near.

Instead he had paymasters for company—to either side of him and likewise shackled up. These were Royalists, known to the camp that held them as Cavaliers—seven in all, and officers besides. Each wore hair long and curled, with lace collar and cuff. They termed the other side Roundheads, for short hair, drab clothes, and glum faces. But that enemy had won the day and there was nothing mumchance about them. The king's men glanced about to a shabby merriment. Dissenters, agitants, hog farmers, tapsters, louts, raff in pot helmet, russet coat, and buff, happy as could be.

This army and its Soldier's Catechism had not long been in use. When treachery, as Parliament saw it, had broken out a second time, no kind thought was left for old means of command. The Royalist captains found themselves doubly unwelcome—not only foes, but a caution to the rest. Jeers and the odd clot drew wit, or a best try. "They haven't even put a man of quality in charge," one Royalist said to the nearest other, over the droop of Vanderas's head. "I can't say much for the new model."

"Any cutthroat may lead," his friend offered back.

The first captain smiled. "Oh, you know, a cutthroat has his place."

No sign of heed from the butt of the remark. Such a rowdy would never be exchanged, and not just for taste. Uncommon though they were in this civil war, foreigners were sure now for the rope. The Count Palatine of the Rhine had left a poor case—nearly as bad as the damp odor of the man set here between them.

Roundheads were not above a stink, but they kept camp in good repair, even on such thankless mud. No other regiments of their army put up tents, preferring to quarter in houses. But the Northern Association had to keep a front where few walls stood. Any houses were left to officers. Not in care for rank, but to keep maps dry.

Officers—a necessary vice, though some did earn esteem. In rode one such now, to a cheer that spread. This was Colonel Stephan Makepeace. He oversaw the horse and, through his lieutenant colonel, Harold Calloway, the halfpike and musket. In that crowd of the Godly the colonel struck a handsome figure—strong-jawed, dark of brow. Above the stirrup no drop of mud dared touch his Puritan cloth. Despite his sect he drew loyalty, and even the most radical of Levellers liked how quickly he had sorted out wages. But the colonel had not long been in the field, and none could say how tactics might have come to him. Makepeace's post in the hostilities two years back had been under the scoutmaster-general. Little marvel in that—the new leader of the association had been there, too, and once chosen to replace Sydnam Poyntz had brought favorites along. Back offices were unlikely ground to prove a role abroad, and under fire, but Makepeace had won many a day. Including this one, slow though the hours had gone, witness to horrors in what remained of the nearest town.

Even those shackled captains knew whom the cheer was for. "Well well," one said. "A man of celebrity." Release, once paperwork was signed, now stood close. The man of worse repute threw a cough and spat.

Hat and helmet off, the Roundheads made a lane. Makepeace met the triumph with a prim smile, never too close to a sin of pride. Next rode his guard—a detachment of elite dragoons from Okey's ranks, outfitted with saber and doglock carbine. Behind those six were two others—and no warrant or commission could account for them.

First was a man in jet cloak, with a deep hat of the same dye and a muffler scarf about the face. Only eyes showed atop, pale and serene. Second was a woman, with red locks and a green hood drawn tight. The man was the colonel's aide, addressed only as Sentance, with no first name aside of mister. He was known to carry an unusual blade and a brace of pistols—odd for a valet, and none took him for such. The woman was another thing yet, and gossip was more open. In any camp the regiment struck she came and went unannounced, her attentions aloof, and the horse and foot saw a harlot. Makepeace's or his man's—none could say—but they did look on her with disfavor and, no less often, a wish.

The cheers led to the command tent. There, presented at the flap, stood Harold Calloway. He and Makepeace had fought their men from separate quarters and they had not seen each other since scheming out the battle. Calloway was twice Makepeace's age, weathered into a squint, and Scottish except in loyalty. He had come up by the usual means, through years of war at home and in foreign parts. A seasoned vet, but he showed no brusqueness to the man above him, lately an ink-pusher. In truth he took off his hat. A silence fell as Makepeace stepped up.

"Well met, colonel," the old Scot said. "I give you joy."

"The victory belongs to all. Strike the barrels, lads— let's take a drink."

Hoorays again as the commanders embraced. Six dragoons made a double file as Makepeace and Calloway went through the flaps. Sentance was close behind— furtive and quick—and none looked to him save with a glance and a superstitious thought.

The woman's horse had come to a stop, this near a sergeant. Few had seen the face beneath the hood. But to displease a man far from home it would have to have been sour indeed. Help her down, a sure go, the sergeant thought, and he put up a hand. He got what he hoped for—sight of a comely face, pale and lightly freckled, with eyes a vivid green. Yet the stare held such venom that it pushed him back.

Both her slippered feet hit the ground at once, and her skirts dropped to the mudded calves. Róis Nimhiúil na Rua was the full name Makepeace and others knew her by. Venom Rose, more or less—no small feat of phrase in a culture left without snakes—and "the Red." This name had once been a matter for the docket, and now it was a joke. None else spoke Irish there, and the English made guesses at the meaning. To them she was Róis for short, or, as they liked to maim it, "Rosh." Her true name was Sadbh, and only one voice would ever say it to her again.

\* \* \*

Paired braziers kept the tent lit and warm, and a skylight vent let the fumes escape. Two tables had been set up—one of good length, centered for conference and a map, the other to a side. Presently the latter was heaped up with spoils—weapons, or those too good for scrap or sutler. Makepeace and Calloway went to the map, and Sentance to a corner by the entry.

"Lancashire is secure," the Scot said, finger to parchment. "The last are holed up at Clitheroe."

The colonel smiled. "A granary, all but. Three hundred could bait there, maybe, but without room to share a pisspot. Scarcely any threat to us."

Róis came in last. She was not unaware of the occupied corner and kept her gaze down, going to that opposite. There she took out yarns and a pair of hooks.

"No sign as yet," Calloway went on. "No loyalists from the north. Perhaps the Presbyterian regime did its part."

"Doubtful," said the colonel. "And not just for a fickle lot. But here's news: Wooldridge sent a messenger. He's coming out in person." Head of the association, with immediate report to Black Tom Fairfax himself. Presently he was northeast, in a sprawling fortified camp of three regiments, artillery included.

Met with cheer, that report, but only by Calloway. Sentance did not attend. His thoughts had gone to the cache on the table. He crossed the floor, pulling down his scarf to inspect what he had spied amid the heap. The face shown was pleasant, and more—though cold of eye, a trifle gaunt, perhaps angelic.

15

"To the frontier, then, to marshal forces?"

"I don't know, Harry. I couldn't say what brings us to these parts—Wooldridge knows better than us. Horton and Old Ironsides, they had reason to end up where they did. But farther north is a mystery. Our friend will ride ahead of his men. His second, Miles Jacobs, is coming too. You know him, do you not?"

"Aye—that mischief at Edgehill. We both lost a piece. Though mine's less plain."

Calloway was about to hold out the keepsake—a thumb taken at the knuckle—when a blade was drawn at his back. He and Makepeace turned hard on the rasp. None saw Róis clutch at her needles. All her focus was now on Sentance. In one hand was a naked blade. The other showed a baldric of knives and the scabbard for the sword. Drawn for a look, the weapon confirmed some notion, and Sentance gave Makepeace a nod. For vantage the colonel stepped up close.

"That?" Calloway said. "It belonged to a mercenary. A foreigner, and a bloody bastard—he was no end of trouble. But we have him alive, praise our luck."

Sentance had leaned to Makepeace's ear. At the rustle of his voice Róis broke her stare, gone white, and she fumbled at the yarns. The knot built, and the colonel gave a smile. "This steel won't break or rust or lose its edge. A lost art from a place we've no names for. Harry, you don't realize whom you've caught, but this weapon, this is sure. Joaquim Vanderas. Notorious, and even aside that I know you've heard of him. It was he who did the enemy's work at Gaddis Bridge."

16

A report five years old. Calloway's face showed the pains. "He took of that loss."

"Took himself," Makepeace said. "And left many with a reminder." Both men had friends who wore the scars—among them Jacobs, Wooldridge's second.

"I'd thought it rumor, no more, that a lone man could do so much."

The whisper again. Makepeace turned back to Calloway. "Come," he said. "Let's have a look at the prisoners."

Intent on the snarl in hand, Róis did not watch them go. But she had seen the anger plain in Calloway, the welcome in Makepeace. The third man—no, there never was a read to be had of him. Róis was damned, she knew, and had long since parted ways with the mother church. Yet she made the cross once Sentance. last out, had left the tent. That monstrous whisper, heard so often at an ear—even close to her own.

The approach sat the Cavaliers upright: terms were near. Roundheads parted and here he was, the famed commander, with aide and second close behind. He stood with a stern eye and said nothing. The Cavaliers became uneasy at the silence. But he was looking not to any one of them. The hireling never gave back the stare, nor took notice. The shiver had grown worse.

It was the Scot who stepped out to address the soldiers. "Who among us knows nothing of Gaddis—the work done there? Who knows nothing of the man who toyed with our brethren, and who cut upon the wounded even as they lay down arms? Today, on this ground, so hard won, we've found him who need answer!"

With a rumble of voices every last eye in those companies had gone to the hire. The Scot brought his face down to Vanderas's line of sight. Either Royalist to a side thought to speak, then better. Beneath the red hat the chin rose, attention shown at last—with a face white from more than weather. Red eyes, teeth in a chatter.

"Why tremble?" Calloway said. "Wisnae this the name you made?"

No more than a grin came in reply—crazed, sick— but contempt spoke.

The Scot put back a hand, but Makepeace came up behind to block the swing. "It's for drink he shakes, Harry, and only that. You wouldn't have caught him otherwise. Those king's men—their stores must have run dry." To the Roundheads he gave a more public voice. "Friends—we'll have justice, be sure of that. But weigh you this. For all his doings—the costs of that day—this man was bought. And what was it that paid the bill? The royal chest. Charles Stuart, that man of blood, and his fat underlings. And those who offered wages have done so yet again. Such men can only share the crime. The stain is theirs as well, and the debt." To Calloway he said, "Clear a space. Have the halfpike form a circle. Unchain the captives. Arm them."

Done, in turn, and a crate of basket swords was brought near. The mutter of the crowd was up yet again, to a circus atmosphere. Rare, for sure—to arm prisoners of war—and here and there a laugh spoke through.

Sergeants had knelt to undo the chain and the Cavaliers leapt to their feet swift enough to bowl them down. Shiver aside, Vanderas had not yet moved. But the Royalist captains took little heart in being so close. Makepeace and Calloway had gone just outside the ring of pike.

"Colonel, I protest!" said a Royalist.

"An honorable surrender!" said another. "You are obligated with our safety."

"None of this army shall harm you," Makepeace said. "You might go free in truth, and without exchange. All you need do is best a single man. Seven on one: fairer than you were with the common folk in town. Mark you all—fairer by far."

The swords were thrown in, yet in their pack of straw—several for the Royalists and one for their pet. Taking up arms, the two nearest captains stood off as far as they might, and the pikes came up to goad them back. The others fell into a huddle.

Calloway leaned to Makepeace. "I'm not easy with this. They should be tried."

"They are being tried. On my conscience, Harry, mine alone."

Vanderas had stirred—a glance to the nearest weapon. His eye found the colonel but he made no move for the muddy hilt. The knot of Royalists trembled.

At last Makepeace gave a nod. To Vanderas he said, "I could no more set you free than speak a lie. But I do know your need—your thirst." Sentance had come up behind with a ceramic bottle—the contents plain enough, even through the clay. He set it to the colonel's hand. In his left grip Sentance held the customary gear—the baldric, the backsword. And this was where Vanderas's notice had truly fallen.

Makepeace held the bottle up. Vanderas looked to it, to the colonel, with a smile. Soon enough he stood in a hunch, took up the basket sword, weighed it. A silence fell. The crowd held breath. The Cavaliers' eyes were fast to the opponent, weapons up. A shift forward, and a full step back.

No mind for that gaggle, not for Vanderas. The weapon in his hand earned a frown, no more, and a toss gave it back to the mud. So unarmed, he spoke straight to the colonel, with a back to the Cavaliers. His English was fair but inexact, and the accent was thick. "My own. Give it here. Yes?"

Makepeace looked to the gear in his lackey's keeping. "Why?"

"For laughs, let's say—for the fun. Come, English. Be sporting now. You wouldn't bait a bear with a nanny-goat. Not where you hope to please a crowd."

The colonel thought on it. His man took the nod and came forward. The muffler was back up, but even with so little shown, Vanderas searched the features.

"You there. We have met?"

No hesitation: a gloved hand hooked the cover free. The face above the loop of scarf told nothing, gave nothing, but Vanderas seemed on the verge of recognition. Sentance only waited, staring back, for whatever decision would become necessary.

The best chance, the only. A Royalist captain—he who had sat to Vanderas's left—took a step out. The captain's fellows were more circumspect, and they held to their patch of mud. He looked to the Roundheads surrounding, all of whom kept still.

And desperation had brought that captain near indeed before Sentance made good. He drew the backsword and gave a throw—underhand, to a catch and a pivot, fluid and fast.

Gone high, the basket sword, and high yet as the man who held it staggered back. The throat sprang open. Sinews in the wound shimmied like a strum. Blood caught up to the cut, all of it, and he reached to stop the mortal spurt. But horror grew faint and the touch fell short. Knees first, then prone, a last heave before going still.

The mutter was angry, but not so angry as the Royalists. "Bastard!" said one.

Said back, "A cutthroat has his place."

At an amble he came on. Tissue was flicked from the blade with a snap. Deft, but once out of play Vanderas looked unformidable again, a rainy wretch. Step and stance showed no sign of readiness. He coughed as the Royalists fanned out—a new circle inside the one that held them all. Vanderas stood center to both.

Voices among the Roundheads had quit. Churchly silence, even a churchly devotion, but no study was so close as that of Colonel Stephan Makepeace.

Another cough took Vanderas. He looked to the points of the swords about him. His own was slung shallow, loose in hand, almost touching to the mud.

"Well?" he said.

The noose sprang shut. And what came brought a gasp from all who never saw it. The afterimage drawn outlasted the deed—ribbon that broke where men had stood. All six Cavaliers fell to a new circle. Every wound dealt out was mortal. Yet Vanderas seemed hardly to have shifted a foot. He held the ground, hunching over to work up a stubborn phlegm, and there was no other show of strain. But the sleeve on the sword arm was red to the elbow, a tinge growing light in the drizzle.

Marvel all around—even on a widower of the field such as Harold Calloway. The colonel stood in shock as well, though passing. Only his aide was unmoved from a taut dispassion—though he, too, was intent.

Vanderas turned to Makepeace. "Well?" he said.

The colonel stepped just inside the pike. A bland smile, a toss. Snatched up and unstoppered with the teeth—but Vanderas took no draft. The clay went out to arm's length, and mud drank the stream. A shake, a last drip, and the jug let fall.

Makepeace's surprise was plain, and the crowd fell silent.

Vanderas said, "It all pours the same." And he made straight for Makepeace.

The colonel stepped back as pikes came up. Every Roundhead soldier took arms. "Hold!" Makepeace shouted. His deputy had come forth, and the pike made way.

Sentance drew. What he held ready was a strange heirloom. No man there save the one who held it knew of an odachi, or even of the realms that spoke the word. Backcurved, with refold steel and a double hilt bound in cord of shark. Once swung from horseback for a noble clan, it had become a totem, kept in a special room until stolen from the rack. Any eye of western Europe could only find it alien, more so even than the long knife that Vanderas held. Calloway's awe said no less.

"What manner of—"

The remark went unfinished. Sentance leapt. Vanderas brought up his guard, but just, and the fight threw a flurry.

Swords flashed in the billows of mud, and the two men beat like rags at a gust. Sentance drove Vanderas back to the center. Eyes in a lock, there they parted.

Astonishment, dead silence, save for the pant of the combatants. Sentance's breath was deep and even, Vanderas's rough.

"My God," Calloway said. "Oh my God."

Sentance and Vanderas kept weapons up and wide, mindful only of each other. That is until the halves of Vanderas's hat slid free. He looked to pieces at his feet and touched at his scalp. No blood, no sting, though a few hairs stuck.

"We couldn't have met," he said. "I'd remember a fair duel."

"Fair, eh." That voice, so rarely spoke aloud, was resonant and deep and carried without volume beneath the murmur of the crowd. "You're feverish. I won't take advantage."

Such tact could only draw a sneer. The opponents pounced, to a blur. Faster yet—the work crossed the circle, to and fro, and neither could gain advantage. Makepeace watched, watched, took it in, silent as the rest.

They parted as a fit of coughs overtook Vanderas. He fell to a knee, spat, coughed again. Mud had caked him to the shoulder, and it slid off in clots. Sentance had eased off, back a full pace, and he awaited the opponent's eye. Once had:

"Yield."

Anger brought Vanderas up, anger and pride, to a reckless lunge. Sentance laid a gash as he sidled from the charge. Backsword out and high for a block, Vanderas stumbled and came to a stop. The other hand held the cheek, the astonishment clear.

The Roundheads began to cheer their man. Sentance, a mystery in camp, was now its champion. He looked only to Vanderas. Under the noise, he said the contemptible word again.

Vanderas stood, tensing for the pass. But instead he bolted away. In absorption the pike had lowered their points, and two shafts made a fair springboard.

He might have cleared those dumbstruck heads had a rope not snared him. A lasso, in truth—fast to an ankle. Sentance had sheathed the odachi and brought it out from his cloak. Length by length he hauled the catch.

On sight of this something gave. The Roundheads broke ranks and swarmed to the fallen man. Kicks, fists, shouts, abandoned to justice.

Sentance threw down the rope and drew a pistol lefthanded. He fired into the air and the odachi was out again. For once that face was not at ease: with a naked and frightening intensity he leapt among the men.

"Hold!" Makepeace cried out. "Hold there!"

The soldiers reeled clear, clutching spots where Sentance had nicked them—knuckles, wrists, each mark deeper than a hair. Calm had returned to that strange face, though weapons stayed ready. He spoke nothing but the truth:

"Any who steps up is a dead man, hear you, dead."

Beneath him—safe though battered—Vanderas heard only his own sickly gasp. Makepeace had come up. He knelt for the backsword, shook it clean, and showed it to the fallen man. To no understanding, no reply, and at last no wakefulness.

A woman's voice—and soft—in Irish Gaelic made for a good lullaby, especially as sung beside a cottage hearth. But Róis ran the verses only to herself, or to a memory held dear, and the cottage was no happy sort of ruin. A rookery for bats of late and a home for mice, long out of upkeep. Her knitting had grown worse—no sense to the tangle, no article in mind, but wherever she was brought to, those needles came out.

Presently at the side of this sickly diego, laid atop a cot. This had been put in the room just for the purpose— one of the only warmish rooms for miles all around, and the other two were just past a door. Beneath a mothy plaid the man was not only nude but nappied. She had bathed him with a wet rag and no small pains, and he and the blanket were both tied down under lengths of rope. The quartermaster had brought a chair for Róis, but she showed none of the gratitude dreamt up. In the hearth itself was another chair, this one broken down to feed the flames. Heat was a godsend, and whatever the sight of it in that fire glow, the room was dry. The eyes had kept shut for quite a time—no sound past a breath, not a word, from the feverish man.

So it caught Róis off guard when he made a try. A wrist had come free but the reach, for her needles, fell short. Bonds held the elbows as well as the chest, waist, knees. Perhaps another loop would do about the neck, she thought, though that was only a matter of time. A yank, tips outward, had brought the hooks clear of his hand and his sure death. Sooner, that was.

"On sóc? On està aquest lloc?" Some diego tongue.

"Try the English. We have as much in common, I fear me."

"L'angles? Who are you?"

For delirium he spoke it well enough. Róis gave a smirk. "Your nursemaid, through no want of my own. Likely you'll never know how funny that is."

"Untie me or els llops es mengen las tetas."

"Such pluck for an invalid. El syops can menge as they like. Wetting yourself without remorse for two days now, so you've been. The trots were done before we met, praise to Christ. Even a godless slayer will catch the baby grippe it seems."

"Puta brut. Filla de merda." His lolling eye fell on her lap, the snarl there. Puzzlement and not a fright, but a wild stare all the same.

"Your fate," she said, needlework up. "It's in my hands."

A fight, a sag. "Més tard," he said, going out again. Not that he had truly been there. Fever had a way of bringing out madness in the soundest of men, and this was another sort. Róis considered the gape, the pull of breath, no blame in her eyes.

Tossing the yarns aside she rose. The hooks were tucked away into a sleeve hidden on her dress, leather lined with a mesh of brass. No risk of a scratch.

Before a larger hearth in the other room, Makepeace was at his precious charts. The colonel was not alone—never alone, but now with more than that shadow lurking in a nook. Calloway was with him. Makepeace asked for the room once Róis came in. On a bow Calloway left. Sentance did not. Of course—nor did he stir.

"Awake?"

"What passes for charm in Spanish parts. Aye, awake, though not in his wits. Give it a night, so I'd say. I never did sign on as a nursemaid."

"No—you were blackmailed. This man is important to us. No less so than you."

"Your men take me for a slattern—that's irksome enough. Now you'd have me play the saint. Care for the ill, that's no calling of mine."

"You had a child once, did you not?" Makepeace found a kinder tone once she had turned away. "A fighting man like that—saints are a horde by comparison and for our purposes less valuable."

"Your purposes," Róis said. She glanced to Sentance and found him looking back. She met the gaze but faltered and left.

Makepeace had returned to the map. He spoke as if to himself or a vacant room. "A fever. Only a fever. But he's a sot and well known for it. Why not take the drink?"

"Ask."

* * *

Strife done with for a time, the regiments had dropped stakes about that lonesome country roof. The cottage stood beneath the wind in a small vale, where a scrap of rock churned out a fresh and flowing spring brook. The soldiers would forgo a march, the companies were told, for several days at least. Spirits had grown heavier despite beer and clean clothes and a rest, and even in spite of victory. Hardship seemed yet with them. There were mutterings about the prisoner in that house—a prisoner given comforts that none of them could share.

Still, when guests rode into camp the next day, the foot and horse took heart. The visit was no surprise: the colonel had ordered best clothes, drum and fife, and ranks at inspection. From all that nicety a cheer rose up to greet the party in their saddles. First and foremost Clifford Wooldridge, general of the Northern Association, lately integrated into the new model. He was a seasoned commander—short-shanked and gray, poll and beard alike, but undiminished and with a gentle eye. He wore plate over buff like the horse though he oversaw the foot as well and artillery besides. Off came his hat and freely, even gladly, he returned the smiles.

At Wooldridge's flank, and in front of another detachment of dragoons—Okey's men again—was his friend and camp adjutant, Captain Miles Jacobs. He

28

was a dark-haired man, come up from the trained bands of London-town, and known for cheer—albeit ugly. He wore a townsman's clothes and more notably a simple black patch atop a socket. The blow that had claimed the eye had also laid a seam from hair to chin. Above that scar a lock had gone white, and since he was no Dissenter, like most in that army, he grew it out to a thunderbolt. In truth his head seemed to have been cleft by lightning strike and cherished whole again.

That he could survive so bad a wound made his fiber plain. Even more to his credit, his aim had improved to something heroic. For this he kept a snaphaunce slung to his back, one of a very unusual make. Rifle-gun kept company with a basket sword and a brace of pistols on his belt. War had not left him pretty, but when a fight got brisk his comrades found him welcome—no less so than his jest.

Near the cottage the lane was clear of Roundheads. There, opposite the music, waited Makepeace and Calloway. They too had doffed hats, but not Sentance, who stood behind. A soldier of the foot held the bridle for Wooldridge. He dismounted, and Makepeace gave a bow. "We bid you welcome, General."

"Let's not stand on ceremony." The two embraced. Amid the rah the general spoke to Makepeace's ear. "Stephan, there is much to discuss."

"Mayhap with a smoke?"

"That custom loathsome to the eye," Wooldridge said, to share a laugh. They went inside, Sentance close to heel. But Calloway stayed out for Jacobs. "Bless me," the latter said, "it's good old Harry! I trust you've been well?"

"Better at times, Miles. Though never doubt it's good to see a friend."

"What is it? You look like you caught a wart in prayers on a harlot."

Neither was a pious man—rather earthy, both—and Calloway could not help but smile. "Would that it went down so gratefully. There is something to tell you, I find."

And so when Jacobs came in at last—Wooldridge and Makepeace chatting at the hearth, each priming Jamestown weed with a twig from the coals—he did so with a look of disbelief. He glanced about, noted the door to the next room, and no sooner took it. Sentance had been watching, and without sound he followed.

In her chair Róis had the aimless knitting up again. With a start she saw Jacobs arrive. Neither knew the other, and he spared no mind to anything but the man behind her, asleep and sick in a truss of rope. She watched the stranger—his lone eye, the decision—and found no surprise that he had set a hand to a pistol in his belt.

Less an urge than a fidget—his stare had a distance, and he seemed not to know where he was. Róis did not care for the duty, but she knew she was there to tend a helpless man. Her hold on the knitting changed. Before anything might have come of it, the devil she knew came up behind, fast without a step. Sentance, likewise, kept watch on Jacobs, waited, cleared a skirt of his cloak. There the odachi hung. The sight wilted her nerve. She looked away. A quiver showed in the hooks.

Whatever they had been, Jacobs gave up the notions. His hand fell from the pistol. Returning to the room where his commander puffed the smoke, he might have taken Sentance for another patch of soot on the wall. In any case he paid no mind to what followed him out. To a corner, pensive yet, and Sentance to his.

"A tidy victory, friend," Wooldridge was saying around the pipestem. "Well those clansmen thought twice."

"It is not the Scottish rite," Makepeace said. "And happily they never did keep much cavalry up that way, so they can't speed in on us unawares. This war is needless. If that scelerate hadn't broken his parole and fled to the isle …" The colonel let the thought go astray. He drew a puff. "Moot now. We'll have done with it."

"Sooner than you think perhaps. Tell me, Stephan—is your army ready? Well rested of the siege?"

"Methinks I hear a turn of gears."

"Stuart's not on Wight. He went the other way—a run for the north. But his people haven't rescued him, not yet. For now he's holed up there in Clitheroe."

The doubt showed even before the colonel spoke. "The smallest fort in all Britain? It amounts to nothing, else we'd have snatched it up."

"The intelligence is sound—well bought. Runt of a fort indeed—and there's the ploy. It's the last station of Cavaliers. Your success caught him unawares. He'd hoped to make Scotland by now, thence to raise more forces. But for now he hides—no choice in it—waiting for them to come serenade us with pipers and body lice."

Makepeace turned the news. The thrill remained hid. "So close," he said. "And a shaky footing. You might have sent word ahead."

"But for snitches—and don't we know the bastards well, we from the scoutmaster. Our fugitive got himself cross-country without a hitch. Think on that. I smell a rat, a cat, and a badger besides. No, Stephan, best we approach from opposite quarters—close the escape." Wooldridge tapped the bowl to the brick. "My army will move to good position, near the shire border. All you need do is bring yours first, from the southwest, and we know the way they'll take. Everything else is mud."

Sentance had straightened up—just enough of a rustle to draw attention. "A moment, Cliff," Makepeace said, and rose. If Wooldridge found the other conference strange—whispers with an underling—he kept it to himself.

But Jacobs did not. On the news, left unmentioned on the road, he had come back to the present. He watched openly.

The colonel returned to the seat and took up his pipe. "You see tricks," he said to the general, "and rightly so. Even an unworthy member will be lent support—and worse, ears and eyes. But two armies that come up on a petty Norman keep—Cliff, it's too much noise. Your prize would steal away."

"True. But I see no other means."

"Here's one. A small party, and the fewer the better. Not for reconnoiter, but secrecy, speed. Three men riding by night."

"So few? They might get all the way to the walls. But then what? Clitheroe is small, but how do three men take a garrison?"

Before the last word was said Makepeace had thrown the pipe, a steep lob. But Jacobs had kept an eye on Sentance since the whisper, and only he saw the speed: a draw, a slash, the point trained back into the sheath as two half-pipes struck the floor. Mirror images, split stem to bowl, the cherries yet lit. The blade shot home.

"The sot-weed never had a chance," Jacobs said.

Sentance glanced up. His muffler smothered up a chuckle. Back to the corner.

"I see our second has volunteered," the colonel said.

"With my blessing, Captain."

For all the awe that feat had not struck Wooldridge dumb, but now Jacobs found himself unable to speak. Go along—of course he should go along. His lieutenant back at the manor camp was no less proficient with the job. Grounds patrols could go on without his say. Still there was a premonition—some turn grown near that he would not like at all.

The general had gone on. "Tell me, Stephan, just who is that man of yours?"

"Sentance. He did some work for us. It was he you chose for Ireland."

A qualm, Jacobs saw—and the general hid it fast. "Your threesome needs but a third, it seems."

Makepeace smiled. "Oh, I'll make do somehow."

"I ride out in the morning," Wooldridge said. "Send the party on the third night, General, and at sunrise follow with the regiments. The timing should be right. Charles Stuart, he is as good as ours."

"Sorry—I believe you misspoke."

"With 'General'? No, it was fair. Reply has already gone back to the war commission—lieutenant-general, to be exact. You've been promoted. Old men need swapping out in due. Oh—I had mentioned it, had I not?"

Makepeace, lately colonel, wore surprise poorly. "Are you making game?"

"Only in how I give the word. Does Calloway keep that Scots water on hand?"

A laugh broke the stare on both sides. The chairs scooted as Makepeace and Wooldridge stood. An embrace, a clapping pat at shoulders.

Sentance had no smiles to show—no congratulations—from under the scarf, and beneath his own wan smile, no less a mask, Jacobs felt the unease grow. Make do, Makepeace had said. The captain stole a glance to the sickbed room, and there he saw the worst.

For his part Vanderas saw it, too, in a dream both old and recurrent. The hour was late enough to be early. The coals in the hearth had gone out and no light showed save for a stroke from underneath the door. There was no need to see the anguish for the sounds made, and struggles made the rope creak. The door came open—light enough to throw shadow from a figure in a cloak and stealth. Hauling against the ties, Vanderas gave a yelp, and in turn Róis let out a shriek.

"Íosa naofa!" she said. "Scare the skin off me." A stoop retrieved the blanket from the floor, and she wrapped it back about herself.

"Who are you?" Vanderas said, in lucid English. "What is this place?"

"God between us. Mare, you said. I heard you from out there. Was it on you?"

"On me? What?"

"The hag, on your chest. Mare. That's not the Irish for it."

A smile built, and the English was better than he had let on before the duel. "The Irish, surely. More superstitious even than those who put the boot on their throats. Bogey man, black dog, screamy washerwoman—hah. Nothing's on me but this goddam rope of yours. 'Mare'—where I'm from, that's mother."

Róis had fallen silent, and he could not make out a face. But at last the titter got out. "Oh, that's precious. A killer as calls for mam in his sleep."

No insult was meant, none taken—to a man so prone to boredom fun was ever welcome. "Strange too," Vanderas said. "I have no thought of—no, not thought. How to say? In mind, from before?"

"Memory."

"Oh. Memòria—almost the very word. No—no memory, not of a mother."

Here the laugh quit. Light would have shown her face go soft.

"You might tell me who you are," he said, "and why I'm tied so."

"Róis they call me. You've been the colonel's prisoner for days now. General I should say. But yes, prisoner—much as I've been to your needs. If you're feeling right, best let the sidhe have its ride fore they drop you from the bough."

"So long as I'm giving rides to shes, what say—" No time for a show of wit, she had left. "Mecagum la fusta," he said, "I'm harder than a tun of nails."

From outside, "You don't need a nurse for it, by Christ."

He listened to the step go off. Though not aloud, he said, "If not nurse, then hostage." Vanderas meant her no harm. Some jokes were a long habit, and only lately had he known any pang of conscience. What he had long taken for wenching had been shown to him as something else, cruel and low, once he had the sense to look. He would never be that animal again. But a chance was what it was. The last strain had loosened up the rope, praises be to nightmares. A tug let out more slack yet.

Soon, naked and furtive, Vanderas stood in the doorway. Out in the larger room a bed of coals gave light from the hearth. The plank door had been left ajar. Perhaps he could make do without a captive, godspeed the lass. He searched the room for any tool. In one corner was the cot where Róis had been. At another was a table, which bore a trove of arms. Lucky that, but Vanderas was disappointed—his own was missing. Still, he would not resent such a turn, and he found a serviceable dagger.

Days had gone by on a back, and with fever. The step was uneasy as it led him to plank door, firm in his sights—and quit altogether as Sentance came through.

What showed of the face held no surprise. The odachi mirrored coals. The free hand offered up a pair of manacles, iron without a shine.

Vanderas weighed the opponent against the choice. The bout the other day, the outcome, would not have made the difference. What little he knew of Sentance, there and then, he could see who had the reach.

Dagger let fall, the wrists were offered up. "Might I die in pants?"

The camp spent a last peaceful night, and save for the watch few were out for dawn. Wooldridge's horse had been fed and saddled, and it stood ready outside his tent. The dragoon scouts had already mounted up. Captain Jacobs, less well slept, was out as well. The general pulled on riding gloves as he spoke. "I know you'd return with us. This mission is of the utmost importance. And there's no greater hand with a firearm—just the thing for potting king's men atop a keep."

"It's a chance for a quick end," Jacobs said. "I'm glad to go."

"Yes, Miles—and I'm no less glad that you won't be among this army." On Jacobs's look the general said, "An uneasy feeling. There's trouble in store for all."

Premonitions are catching, Jacobs told himself. Aloud he said, "Take care overland. Even in peace this country's thick with robbers." And he watched the party trot out. His eye was on them as they rode clear of the vale. Silhouettes put spurs to horse and vanished from the rise. In distraction he had not seen Calloway approach.

"Staying? Forgive me, Miles, I didn't mean to startle you. Business at hand?"

"I'm afraid I can't discuss it, Harry."

So he was not the only one to feel uneasy. But a sound was a surer thing than a gut or an itch—namely a rattle of chain.

Turning to a foe led by rope, Calloway and Jacobs both showed grim satisfaction. Vanderas wore shackles and a shirt, no more, and the noose was at his neck. This did not prevent a smile—arrogance, and no look to either man. Jacobs paid no less mind to Sentance, who held the rope.

"Christian of Makepeace," Calloway said, "allowing a head to clear."

"Better done in front of the men." The treeline took Sentance and the prisoner.

"We all remember the bridge, Miles."

Jacobs turned back. "This is no mob, Harry. It's an army, and a matter of law." And he took hope that his misgiving might have been wrong.

"Sore old bugs like myself," Calloway said, "we leave law to juries. I'm just glad to know a bastard's done."

Cases be made, the bastard was not. Makepeace had risen early and laid out goods atop a rock—new clothes in a

Dissenter's style, boots, a skin, two apples, a loaf, and a nub of cheddar. More, there was the backsword and the knives in the belt.

Beside these he took a seat. "The tall stuff's back that way," Vanderas was saying. "Ah—good morning, English. Out for a show? Better yet"—on sight of the gear—"a duel for sport. Me and the gargoyle here, yes? That's rather Mediterranean of you."

"Sentance," Makepeace said. With no more, the noose came off and the wrists shed the irons. Chain and shackle were thrown as one into the underbrush.

Makepeace held up the skin. "Drink?"

"Never touch it," Vanderas said. "Not anymore."

"It's water. From the spring up a ways. Little wonder somebody put a farmstead up, whatever drove them away."

Puzzlement, suspicion—to a thirst these were nothing. Vanderas took the skin.

"When you're ready there's food. But might I ask—the wine you poured out. Did you lose the taste? Or is it something else?"

Bag drained, it fell on a coughing belch. "Strange," Vanderas said. "I had no love of water, so I thought. Least in a goddam breadsop of a kingdom like this one. Wine, you say. English, there's no strong"—searching again—"memory of the other day, but you're not wrong. Lose the taste? Never. Never once. Wine calls. Every moment, every day. Sings, better said, like a woman down a lane. Yet I take no drop. Small ale perhaps, or that apple stuff Englishes use for baptism. But no wine, no spirits—not for years."

"I've never met a sot who mastered it. Did you find God?"

"Barely escaped the snatching bastard. Cheese. Apple," finger trained to each.

"You haven't eaten in three days," Makepeace said on a toss.

Smacking, wolfing, Vanderas ate down the both, rind, wax, and all, and gave some consideration to the stem before he gave a flick. "Thought I'd never taste food again. Whatever evil you have in mind, I'll say thanks. Bread."

"Eluding God? Pray tell more."

"Left for dead," Vanderas said through a crust and a mumbling gnash. "Then monks."

"Monks?"

"Monks."

Until the swallow Makepeace heard no more. But Vanderas had little to add. Archers had struck him down. On the arrows there had been no barbs, nor even target points. Sight of a man facedown under nine shafts must have made a strong case, for Vanderas was left among the dead. Worse, he had lost a friend in his care.

Bitter, and Vanderas preferred the taste of bread, even the sorry English stuff leavened from barley hulls and river grit. He said only, "I'm a working man. What should I expect? I was arrow-shot many times. Quills enough to shame a porc espí."

"A porcupine?" Makepeace asked. "No, never mind—monks are easier."

"Found me. Come for loot. There was a cloister up the ridge. Smoke drew them just as surely as the rot would draw the flies. Going through my rags they saw I had a little breath. So they pulled the arrows and brought me back, or perhaps it was the other way around. Broth went into my mouth once a day, just a drip. They waited for the change of smell. But two weeks later I woke up to matines. A deep sleep, if that's the word. They told me I wouldn't wake, even on a slap, and God preserve them that I never noticed that. I had missed all the pains of going dry. Awake—and sober." With a remorse, however vague, Vanderas said the word again. "No matter. I hardly knew what to do from there, once I could walk out. So I've done what I did all along, with those tools on the rock. Taken up for wages, though not with the same ... care."

"You methods grew more circumspect?"

Vanderas frowned. He had no more regrets to share. "That's hardly what I said, whatever circumspect means. Forget it."

"You've committed terrible acts," Makepeace said, "and until you were rid of the bottle you never had the wit to question yourself."

The scold was not lost on the truant. "Shame from the hangman? No. Fucks to that, as you chinless pudding-wolves like to say. On with it, please. No doubt the blade is ripe and ready on that black Jesuit of yours." Yet when he turned, Vanderas saw that the two had been left alone.

"Jesuit?" Makepeace said. "He's hardly a man fit for church. Weapons, vestment—in the style of this army. I want you to join. There's puddings enough for everybody." Scabbard and belt came up in hand.

41

"Huh. No surprise. What's puzzling is the ... credulitat. What's the—?"

"Gullibility."

"You would not, should not, cannot trust me. Blood is on my hands—friends' blood."

"And more. Those king's men, turning on them: you enjoyed that."

Even from a weeklong derangement Vanderas could see it well. "They deserved worse, the pampered wretches. I carry on. Your second—where is he?"

"It's a show of trust. Trust given, trust gained."

Sentance had gone to the undergrowth, to crouch with a rifle-gun. Matchless fire—fumes would have given his position even before the sizzle.

"My men will grumble," Makepeace said, backsword and knives held out. "And that's only fair. What's said here is not for them—not yet. Please. Take your arms."

A last hesitation, and Vanderas lunged forward. But he only pulled the backsword and left the rest swaying in the grip.

"You're mad, English," he said at last, glancing about. "Your man's quick, but not this quick."

The rifle-gun did not hold a standard ball, but a tapered ammunition made by a Flemish gunsmith, pricy, rare. Sentance knew the value of straight flight and good aim, and he drew his bead where head met neck.

"There's a spark in you," Makepeace said. "A decency. That's why I ask."

"You ask because I'm a killer without equal. Or without better."

"The Lord provided. Think of the parable of the talents. Matthew, chapter twenty-five."

"Em reserva," with a roll of the eyes.

"Your gift has found no purpose, no use, for you have no enemy."

"English, I've had more than I—"

"Opponents—those were opponents. An enemy, that's something more. Lives have been cheap to you, equally so, and that sets the price on yours. A worthy foe—a purpose—you thirst for it as some might for love. Those Cavaliers—you relished the deed because you know them for what they are. Stooges, like you. Stooges for those who make a misery of this world. The nobles— queens, kings, all the rest—they are despots, every one. Have you ever met a royal worthy of faith, or even of due? Have you met one who wasn't cruel, capricious, incapable of shame—even one?"

Vanderas took time. "One, none—what's the difference."

The finger eased from the trigger.

Makepeace spoke as he might to any veteran. "Who profits from the silver paid out? Stuarts, Bourbons, Habsburg scum. You know what they are as few others might—what they bring. This country is in revolt—the one place in Christendom where eyes are open. Never again shall we abide misrule. Never again will we suffer a tyrant. For all love, set right what you've done. Know the enemy. Where else, when else, than here and now? Consider at least that the coin I pay out is worth no less."

"I do find I need the work," Vanderas said. And Sentance quit his aim. "Your men—they won't like it. Nor should."

"Fight aside them and in time they'll see a friend, a brother. Soon, perhaps, given the import of the mission two days hence."

"Mission?"

"To catch the king of England."

Morning had just begun, but some in camp were out for sight of the late recruit. Vanderas had put on the clothes, all but Puritan, and the general walked aside, Sentance at the rear. Morning chores fell silent as Roundheads took up the stare.

At the cottage Makepeace broke off, speaking to captains who had come up, far from pleased. Vanderas did not sample that grief. Instead he took the grin indoors. Sentance had stayed out, and for the first time in days Vanderas found himself without restraint. He also found Róis, by the hearth in a rickety chair.

She was spooning frumenty up from a bowl. The pot was on the flame, and a steam pecked through wheat and currants. His smile did not go unnoticed. "Welcome to the conspiracy, butcher of men," she said. "You'll find the potty by the bed and the privy hole in back." But the laugh burst out, and she gave a narrow eye. "What's got you so merry?"

Speed was the essence of his talent, so it was no wonder that Vanderas took her off guard. Her face was in his hands; to her frown he laid a kiss. And he was laughing yet as he bolted for the rear and the spoon struck the doorframe, and then the mush.

* * *

Fate would toy with him—that was nothing new. But the chase to come kept funny on to noon. The sloth of several days had got Vanderas antsy, and he took the stirrings out. Behind the cottage a dummy was hung in a tree— a target made of straw put up by the dragoons on their stay. Vanderas had no need for their rehearsals, but sick or whole he did love to fling a knife. So on the baldric went, and he drew fast at twenty paces, again and again. Where eyes might have been, a nose, each tooth, he placed a strike. Sweat was the hope, honest sweat, and he wore no shirt to soak it up.

The spot was solitary but not hid from camp. Glares were lent out in plenty, but only to a back. Vanderas felt the tickle, and whenever he would look Roundheads would study dirt.

Only Jacobs was less cagy. He had heard the news, same as any, but had come on order. Still, he felt astonishment to see it confirmed there behind the cottage—the enemy not only free but fully armed, sporting on the victim.

The turn came, the simper, and the captain held the stare. The smile fell off, and Vanderas walked up to pull the knives, stashing them to loops. Back to the mark, he went again—this time throwing as fast as he might. Twelve blades in a juggler's swoop, riddling the target. It swayed and held to the end of the rope. As it swung back Jacobs saw the work. Handles wrote an X, and the bottom half fell away.

Vanderas turned again, now with a shrug.

Jacobs broke away. At the front of the cottage the posted guard gave salute before telling him Makepeace was in the command tent. There Jacobs found the under-general in conference with officers at a map. "Wooldridge asked that we forgo the scouts," he was saying, "to avoid detection. Instead foot and horse will march out in file, two columns keeping pace."

"General. Sir."

Even with half a gaze the haunted look was clear. A nod cleared the tent. Makepeace said, "I know what you'd say, Captain. As you watched took many lives dear to us all."

"Half blind, too done in to render aid. It isn't mine to ask."

"I wouldn't lead but that I keep a man's faith."

"You have it. But know that were it otherwise, I would call him out."

"That would be sure death, Captain."

"Even so."

"He'll ride with you. So doing he'll earn a measure of humanity."

"Two yard deep, one hopes."

On a bow Jacobs ducked out through the flaps. Makepeace returned to the chart. A brisk step brought Jacobs back to the cottage. He hardly slowed at all, nor even glanced, as he drew a pistol.

The shot cut the rope, and what was left of the straw doll hit the ground. Vanderas had fallen to a crouch. A knife was up and ready. But Jacobs never looked back

46

from the walk. Only the smoke piping from the hand told who.

Vanderas rose and looked to the Roundheads. Now less shy—some chuckling to themselves, others plain with hatred once kept discreet, and none cowed. Later, they would spot Jacobs a cask of ale, glad that somebody could show the bastard up.

The bastard did not mind. He gave a smirk and put the blade in hand to a loop.

Jacobs had made a point of keeping up on Sentance—his errands, his whereabouts—but with his fluster the absence in the command tent had gone unnoticed. Just as unforeseen was the arrival in the cottage. She had been sitting at some peace in the rickety chair, knitting again with a tune sung low. And Sentance reared up from her complete inattention and waited for her eye.

Frozen to the seat, she stared back. A hook was up in a tight grip.

"Aon fiacla, damhán alla?" he said. The voice was soft. "Dare you bite?"

The grip began to shake. Róis glanced to the hook. She let the fist drop.

There was something in his hand, too: a dagger in a sheath. Holding it out, he said, "The potency must last. There might not be use for quite a while."

She took the simple weapon, gaze held low. "Palsy? Blindness?"

"Such love of half measures. Sure death, and fast. On your honor, as it is."

In a sweep he was gone.

Róis considered the blade, the task. Any peace in that briefest moment to herself was gone. For all her precaution, all her care, Sentance could yet take her by surprise.

Dusk fell. Three horses with dark coat had been picked out, and they stood ready outside the command tent. With utmost care a groom, whatever his thought, was putting on livery. The tent and those in the ranks behind took on a glow from lamps within, lamps themselves.

Jacobs was inside, alone, by his own blackout lamp—as Wooldridge's man nominally in charge of the outing, but only that. The clothes he wore were much like the usual in camp, but here even the shirt was black. He strapped the rifle-gun atop the cloak and tucked pistols to a belt. Wherever it could be of use, a silent weapon would be handiest, and Jacobs slung a basket sword to a hip and buckled daggers on the other side. So much tackle, and none of the burden made him feel the safer. Jacobs picked up the lamp. In night they would be crossing pitted moors, and a spot of light would be a mercy to the animals. Country fit for a ghost hound, and doubtless home to one, or to worse, once the skies had guttered out.

In the cottage wreck Vanderas, too, made ready. For him this was a happy rite—no misgiving, only a sense of sport. The backsword could not rust but the roil did grow dim in time. As he ran the cloth he thought about how the weapon's long company. Stains were inevitable, but a rag and oil, these took off the tarnish.

Róis came in.

"A farewell," he said. "What a treat."

"Don't tell me the errand," she said. "None who rides by night is up to good."

"Your master, he didn't say?"

"Makepeace knows the less I hear, the better I sleep."

"As you like, Rosh." He knew the wrong but there was fun in it—a shared distaste for their hosts and the manner of speech. Not without cause French soldiers named English troops as les goddams. And the English themselves liked to call their poets muckspout. "Far be it from me to spoil bedtime. Hah. It'll be quite a story, though. Perhaps the best yet."

"Keep many such, do you?"

"To myself, mostly. Thanks to drink a lot is blank. Yet I know too much. Well ... never mind it." His attention was on cleaning, and she could not see the face he wore.

"Regret, is it, then? Shame even? There's no joy in murder—just a busywork?"

He turned to her, and even before he spoke she saw her mistake.

"Joy," he said at last. "Is that how to put it? What I did, I remember that, but none of what I felt. Joy or worse—and I'm glad."

"Vanderas," Róis said, and close. "Listen now. Don't you run afoul of Sentance."

"The lady cares?" He did not look up.

"Keep it in your drawers. There are many ways to die. Some are terrible—evil."

"Terrible ways. I'm no stranger there."

"I'll say no more." She stepped away but did not leave.

He took this for invitation, and he searched the downcast face. Before now he had not taken in the features. Comely enough, that troubled face, though not untouched by weather. This was not what fixed his interest—no, it was the color of the eyes, the vivid green. And it would stay with him from then on. She was newly met but the eyes themselves—somehow the green of those eyes was not.

That vague welcome got him on his feet, and she shied back.

Unlike for his former self this was enough to make him stop. "No goodbyes then?" he said. "As you like. But I'd know you better if I had the chance."

"'Know' he calls it."

"Few take me for wise. But even I see there's more here than a charwoman."

"And more than you'll be told, Vanderas. Far more," and her voice broke. Heartfelt, that rasp, but followed with a grin that quickly showed it up.

Green eyes and a gallows smile. Here Vanderas felt something new—a warmth he could not name. Years on the roam had left it undiscovered, that or drink.

"Call me Joaquim," he said, near a falter. "That much is the name I was born to." He made to draw close again—this time for sakes other than his own—but Róis left.

Something for a roster, made up on the spot—that was the truth of the fame that had followed him, then led him by the teeth. He had struck his mark aside it many years before—Vanderas, a simple x—and had heard it read back ever since. The name of a coastal village long since taken off the map.

When Jacobs came out Sentance was mounted up. The dress was the same but he had taken down the scarf. Jacobs did not look to that bare face as yet—all his mind was on the enemy. Vanderas was just down from the cottage. Both men were armed to a glut, but Vanderas carried no gun—only the backsword and knives.

"Good evening," Jacobs said.

"Good evening." The tension went without the usual remark. Hardly circumspect—the horse and gear provided, and more so a private thought, had all his mind. The first was a good distraction from the second—a bed roll, panniers, a saddle, and foremost a bow and quiver. English-style, that meant, lashed unstrung behind the cantle. The limbs of the bow flew out a good half yard from the horse's flanks. Few arrows had been stashed in the pocket. Vanderas had not carried any such weapon of late, and since waking in the company of those friars only had a few times. His views on archery had shifted toward the cautious and perhaps even to a superstition.

All he said aloud was, "In gun times? Well, it's your money, Englishes."

"Past the crossroads we take the Bowland Fells." This from Sentance.

"Not much moon out," Jacobs said on a heave into the saddle. "Even with lamps that country goes hard on animals."

"He's not the sort who minds," Vanderas said.

Jacobs gave a glance to Sentance and looked again, this time lingering. "Have we met, sir?"

The stare was duly returned. "No."

Perhaps not, but the calm, drawn face held Jacobs's search until Vanderas brought the shutter open. A beam wobbled on the dirt before the hooves. The captain did the same with his own lamp, looking off, and the scarf went up.

To Vanderas Sentance said, "This is a parole. Don't stray far."

"You needn't finger that trigger," Vanderas said. "Hunt down a king like a rabbit in the grass? I for one am hooked."

At a trot the three rode off, light slashing out the way. Jacobs kept watch for gopher holes, but his mind was yet on a face—and he was not alone in it. Soon the bounds were left behind, the cottage farther yet. By means of loft and unpatched hole Róis had gone to the roof, and she watched the lanterns trace. She had no rosary to count, had not carried a string for years, so the hooks made do once more. Her thumbs worried at the dull ends, and she had no prayers in mind. Yet she stared on. One lamp winked out at the crest, another, the last.

The distraction was shared. Vanderas scarcely kept to the path, and the beam veered to the brush. Her eyes were lit up brighter though he tried to snuff them out.

That she could trouble him so, this sour Irishwoman, was a puzzle. Yet here she was, warning him again, even as what she had warned him of kept a close trot.

Jacobs weighed his own haunted feeling, and surprisingly it had strayed from the killer he knew too well. Sentance had been a mystery since that first night, and now the captain had the face. The uneasiness ran deep. Back in camp he had brought up Makepeace's deputy, only to find that the men liked to let a jinx pass unremarked. The ghost nearby, Jacobs could not deny that he felt it, too. In an hour Sentance called a halt, dismounted, and stood off. The need might have given his companions heart, but there was no relief—no sound of a stream or foam. Sentance only looked out across moonlight sown on the heath. To what, neither could guess.

Two more hours to the crossroads. Rocky figures stood in peat like vanes in a flood. A quarter moon ran a share on the horizon. Many byways kept a gibbet set up, and here it was no different. On a hank of rope swung a ripe form, held together only by the cage. The wind was picking up to drive the lonesome creak.

Sentance raised a hand. "Here on, lanterns out," he said.

"We ought to bait the horses," Jacobs said.

All three came down, damped the wicks, and poured oat to bag. Vanderas's eye had gone to the victim—faint in moonlight though the rope spoke plain. He sought a fresh distraction, and said, "How'd our friend come to decorate the road, I wonder?"

"Likely you have insight," Jacobs said. His horse chomped at the ration.

53

"A bruixot no doubt. What's the English …. This is trying for you, I'm sure."

"Which, sir."

"To ride with an enemy. I don't remember you, but I can read a face."

"Brush up on that English. Though you're less short there than you are on duty. 'Warlock'—that's the word you're after."

Vanderas had set down his bag. "Sentance is gone."

The captain looked in each direction, to nothing much at all. The third animal was yet there. Jacobs shushed Vanderas and listened to the surround—noiseless but for horse breath, and their own, beneath the wind rake and tractions of the noose.

Vanderas said, "Eight in soft boots."

"What?"

Faint struggles, the way unsure—Jacobs turned to and back.

"He's on them," Vanderas said. "Seven now. Five." A patter of soles. "Draw."

One man took up backsword and knife, the other blade and pistol. On came the promised five: dirks ready, the men bent on the horses. The muzzle flash lit up hard faces, and one cried and fell. The rest was done blind. Scant moonlight flashed until a cloud began to steal even that dimmest trace. By ear alone Vanderas cut down three more, and the parting of flesh stood out no less sharply than each gasp and sigh. The last made a sprint, and light died in the cloud.

Jacobs had unslung his rifle and taken aim down the road.

"Curse me," Vanderas said, "where's that bow. You'll never hit at this range."

The captain held steady. A sparking gout threw shadow and was gone with the clap. Darkness returned in the stink of powder.

Vanderas had gone to his horse. English longbows were longer yet than those abroad and had a high draw. Difficult to string, even with lever, and he struggled at the brace of his boot. "He might have friends to warn. I'll take the bastard."

"He's taken," Jacobs said.

Vanderas had a look. The cloud ferried off and sight returned. Down the road, between the old ruts—a hundred yards, more—a heap was shown.

"Not likely," Vanderas said, by way of cheers. "Not goddam likely."

"This gun is more exact than most. A twist in the bore makes the shot fly straight. Rifling they call it."

"What is that drum there?"

"Eight shots—a German design, and not cheap. I'm known for aim, cyclops or no."

"You've outdone me. I've never been good with a gun."

"Odd I should owe a skill to you."

Vanderas's question was cut short. A lamp had opened.

He and Jacobs turned fast, weapons up, though neither was much astonished to see their companion drawn close. Sentance held a bloody saddlebag, and he threw it into the light. The lamp was not his own—a shoddy thing from another man's outfit.

"Highwaymen," he said.

"On foot?" Jacobs asked. "In the north country? I think not."

Sentance gestured to the gear. "I took the horses first. Lest word spread."

"Eight horses without a sound?"

Vanderas paid no mind. He looked to a fallen man—the very first down, had with a pistol shot. "Tricky," he said. "These men, they're Scots. And Scots are out of place, even in a drippy waste so very much like home."

Jacobs shook his head. "Scotsmen—but how could you know?"

"The accent, yes?"

"None spoke."

"One screamed. And they're overfond of the dirk besides. It's like the village mule up there. They're absconders, I'd bet it—army raff. Looking to get by with a farmer's stolen cabbage and perhaps a turn with the sheep."

Sentance was looking to the dead. The frown was plain and, on that staid face, unusual. Neither he nor Vanderas was sure of the stakes, it seemed. Jacobs looked between them. One was a sot and the other a riddle, but neither was a fool.

Perhaps he was no less a fool. He had no better guesses to the visit. "The keep," he said, "it's three hours yet. We'll need to beat the sunrise."

"Let's not waste the dark," Sentance said.

The moon rose yet higher. Deep heather and gritstone marked the way—soft, then a monolithic thrust. The last hour saw a wide but shallow bog. There a forest edge had drowned and the water gave up snarl and stump, bleached to bone, hardly stirring in the trot. The wind had gone flat, and in short time the riders met up with live tree, and thick. The brake gave cover but left them blind once more. Fetlocks met low switches, and the ache made the horses nicker. As they drove through higher twigs lashed at the men's faces.

Even in that test, and with eight highwaymen still a puzzle, Vanderas thought on Róis. He took the gush uneasily. Any other man would know he was smitten, but he had never felt the like—a pull that had never let up, grown taut in the ride.

They came out just above the Ribble Valley. Low fog hid the watercourse, and the sky purpled to the east against a hoard of stars. Rooftops stood in the blanket and less than a mile out a hillock broke free. Trees had been cleared from the motte, and the block of the keep stood atop. There a single light shone.

Sentance had brought the saddlebag along. As he explained the use to the captain, Vanderas kept a moony vigil on the way they had come.

"God's death," Jacobs said to him, "may we have a moment?"

"Ah? Yes, yes, storm the keep, derring-do, all of that. I shouldn't suppose there's a better way than to blow kisses at the murder holes and ask a dance."

"Heed you now," Sentance said. He had drawn with a stick in the dirt, and the selfsame brush made for a pointer. "Outer wall. Inner wall. From gate to keep the way is circuitous. But just outside there's high rock: shorter than the wall but tall enough for a line of sight."

"You want to fire on them?" Jacobs asked. "Tinker up a catapult?"

Tinker-work had been done in advance. From his cloak Sentance took out a grappling arrow. These were not unheard of, but his was high-grade steel and well machined. Blunt-tipped, spring-triggered, with a second clamp at the back and two eyelets, one on the clamp arm, one at the fletching.

Before Vanderas could ask Sentance had already given it over. A palm dandled it. "End-heavy—an awkward shot."

"Yes," Sentance said, "but well within your fame. Aim for the tower—the garderobe vent."

"Pull a rope in flight?" Jacobs said. "Line thin enough couldn't take a man's weight. And what would you do aside from that, shinny up? Lend a creeping target to the watch?"

Sentance had brought out a coil. Thin-braided hemp, or something like it, dyed to a black. Vanderas ran a fingertip. "What is this made of?"

"The Spaniards fetch it overseas," Sentance said. "No braid is stronger. At the ends you'll see a thinner cord, inside the kern." And he explained how to tie the inner line and splice the foreign hemp to the eyelet.

"Why so busy?" Jacobs asked. "Bodices come friendlier than this."

To nothing. "For your faces," Sentance said, with a jar. "Skin stands out on dark clothes."

Jacobs was a London man and knew of mummer's cork. "You want us taken for Othello?"

To nothing. "As for the rest ..."

The saddlebag held a grouse, it seemed—the red sort from the fells, very much alive. How Sentance could snare a bird in the dark, in proximity to a sneak attack, was kept to himself. But that breed had a feisty way, and rather vocal. Whence the name perhaps, Jacobs thought. The snug fit had kept this one at peace, but the leather quaked from its outrage. He had been sent with the bird to a low position in the fog. There he held the bag unbuckled. Film smeared to his face, he wondered at his role in things.

For theirs Sentance and Vanderas were atop the granite. Vanderas, too, wore the cork, and Sentance had the scarf up. A dwarf tree held a grip on the lichenous stone and its boughs gave them camouflage where they looked to the ramparts. The longbow had been strung, the grapple nocked, and a coil lay ready to spool out. In hand Sentance had a small crossbow—not the deadliest toy, but quiet. He had put a winch block, also quite compact, on the base of the tree. Vanderas had a private thought, that the cloak wore no man beneath, but only device on device that kept the shape—a notion meant only as a joke that instead brought disquiet.

The wall was embattled, and a sentry passed the crenels. Sleepy, bored, not a little fat, he was inattentive to the countryside. He reached the far end and came about again, reeling through a yawn. Behind him was the keep, and the stingy target.

"Hope nobody's on the pot up there," Vanderas said to himself.

Sentance put the crossbow down and raised a hand to Jacobs. "Make ready," he said to Vanderas, with the other poised to his shoulder.

The draw was a toil—a fifty pound push against the wood, with fifty to the pull. Once the tension was highest Vanderas relaxed the grip. The missile rested on his finger, and he fine-tuned the aim. The weight felt urgent—nary a shot in five years, and now a shrovetide stunt. Horn had softened on his fingers and he felt the cut.

Below them Jacobs put a hand to the flap. The other held the belly of the bag. Inside the grouse shifted as if for the cue.

Rounds were no hurry for the man there on the wall. As Vanderas felt the ebb of strength—a burn in his shoulder—at last came the end of the beat. The sentry paused, looked out, dug a nostril, and Vanderas wished him deeper berths in hell.

At last he turned for the sleepwalk back.

The signal fell. Jacobs heaved the bag. A throaty fluster, uncannily human. The captain dropped to mist and hid his smutted face. The wingbeat pattered on the wall.

Vanderas felt the tap. With a last fret the missile flew. No need for doubts at that subtle lash as the line fed out—the shaft wobbled in flight but kept true. Down it came to the distant hole. No sound of the strike, and no sound of the hook sprung.

"And?" Vanderas asked under breath, with a shrug.

No answer, save in what Sentance did next, taking up the slack in hand. The sentry never saw—in search of the voice he had run to the far end. The grouse cleared the wall, and he leaned out between crenels to search the mist below. His gaze fell near Jacobs but without notice. The kit call was already set to his mouth, a tag of iron played like a reed. This, too, had been a device given out for the task.

A cattish yelp: the sentry gave a frown, but he broke off to resume the circuit. By then Sentance had primed the winch. No sound of ratchet, only a smooth crank. The line came tight. Vanderas studied the methods without guessing what Sentance had in mind—a pair of felt soles strung to the boots, a sticky vial there applied. Puzzling, but hardly a wonderment—not until a hop put Sentance on the line.

There he stood, crouched low, and began to pace up the incline. Impossible, yet done, and for once it was Vanderas who was left in a gape. In hand was the odachi, sheath and all, and Sentance held it at the midpoint behind his neck, ends level. Like beam scales, Vanderas saw, something from a merchant's shop. The strand creaked but held. That itself was a marvel, so strong a fiber, but nothing to the feat.

Jacobs had allowed himself a look. In awe he rose up from the mist.

Quick ascent, to a point above the walkway. Daylight would have thrown shade on the walk. And it was there that the sentry came to a halt. Snapped awake—trouble sensed, and near. He glanced all about but never upward. Sentance held a crouch, faintly wobbling on the cord. No spring to the line—no means to pounce far.

Vanderas nocked an arrow. Felling a man from the tops of a wall was a risk. The best of shots could end in a cry, and a body smiting ground was plain even to the deafest of codgers. He watched, kept aim, held a curse ready.

Mind on the surroundings—everywhere else—the sentry came beneath the line. Jacobs fell to haunches and unslung the rifle. Neither he nor Vanderas need have worried. Sentance's poise was a thing to behold, and the right hand sought the hilt.

The sun chose this moment to break, and the first unreflected light of an awful day fell squarely on those watchful eyes. The sentry felt the stare, and at last looked up. On his start Vanderas loosed as Sentance dove. Missile and acrobat struck as one. In truth the shot went into the folds of the cloak, and Sentance dropped out of sight.

Mouth set hard, the archer looked on. It would not have been the first murder of an ally, but accident, that went against pride. But Sentance rose from the merlons. Held up in show was the arrow. Scold hinted as he threw it out, whole and unbloodied and whole. The same hand beckoned, and he vanished again.

A slash, and the backsword took the line at the winch. The strength rang up Vanderas's arm, but the fiber gave. The fray sprang clear and he caught up the end as he sheathed the backsword. Fast, thoughtless: a leap took him out into the air.

Folly, a suicide, Jacobs thought below. Yet he saw Vanderas haul fast. The rope grew short and swung him to the wall. Bouncing on the pads of his feet, again, he reeled in the line, and before Jacobs knew it he was running for an empty length.

Vanderas clambered over. The sentry had a cut to the throat, he saw, and gave reproaches to a spread of blood. Prints made a trail from the pool. Vanderas listened to the yards below. No cries, no alarm, not even the boot that left the mark.

It unnerved him, that early morning silence: his hearing was better than most. But there was nothing told. He made quick to a tread stair, and at its base he found another Royalist slain. The track was rewetted and ushered him to the barracks. There Vanderas made out a lone dull thud. He drew the backsword and ran.

Jacobs had made the top, to the same grim sights. Noting Vanderas below, the route, he readied his gun and ran the opposite way. A stair would lead him down, he saw. He could flank the enemy, perhaps render aid to the man he wanted dead.

Rays sifted through the shutters—bright enough to let Vanderas see the aftermath. He stepped among the bunks. Mosts were empty, but eleven men were there, or no longer. Each had lain asleep and each had a gash to the neck. Volumes had splashed about the bedrolls and even to the undersides above. One man was twitching yet but even he had not woke. Vanderas felt cold bead his face.

Jacobs came down a stile. No enemy—no commotion in the compound, nothing. He and Vanderas met in the middle, and either was so ready for trouble that they squared off. Meeting eyes, and perhaps with reluctance, the guard fell.

"Where is Sentance?" Jacobs asked.

"Something is wrong. The fort is undermanned, royal or no."

"There is no royal here!"

Sentance had shouted from inside the small keep, and he flung wide the oaken door. Even for the black of his clothes blood was evident. It glistened on him like an oil seep. He had taken down the scarf, a frightful intensity on his face, and he ran the odachi into the sheath. "And now, what few there were," he said, coming down the stone flight, "none else."

Jacobs shook his head. "A skeleton crew. Only a call to the field could short a garrison. But there's been no fight this far out since the city fell."

"The Scotsmen," Vanderas said. Sentance had seen the truth already and ran for the gate, the horses beyond, but even in dread Vanderas hesitated to tell Jacobs. "Dressed up for stealth, like us. Not thieves. Scouts."

Beneath scar and patch the captain's face went pale. "Wooldridge is too far."

He ran, and Vanderas, as horror built. Lost to the task, Róis had been gone from thought for an hour or more. But here she was again, atop a horse at her rueful knitting as the trap grew close.

\* \* \*

The designated spot was a wooded stretch of the easting road. Someone who knew the countryside and who had talent for ambush had chosen it. That person was neither there nor far, but the man put in charge kept an eager watch. Manus Ciotach was how fame knew him, not a name of birth but an epithet. In the Vulgate and the Goidel tongue it meant left-handed, and inelegantly, though he was not. None could dispute him a master of war-for-hire, though, a minor chieftain under the Gordon clan. Whiskers were laid deep, black and shaggy, and a claymore was in reach that he liked to think an Englishman could scarcely lift. Some of these southern weeds were in his company—Stuart men from the post at Clitheroe. On arrival the prior day he had disabused those officers of notions that they led.

There was other company, too, and better, in the form of a Gallowglass regiment, so-called. The term had once applied to mercenaries of Norse stock, but that heritage had thinned out enough to make it honorary. Yet for sale, though—men who, like Manus, worked for a living, and half a thousand no less. They too were clansmen, many in Gordon cloth. Not a uniform, but they were disciplined all the same and, despite allies times forced them to keep, hankering for a share of outland blood.

Bows would be the first volley, guns second. Powder smoke would mask the charge. Scouts had reported a double cavalcade, with the general in the center. They had also seen a woman just at his flank, among the dragoons. A camp-follower, for sure; in any case fair game. Manus ordered the column heads taken out first. This was against instruction from higher up—it had been clear that the young general was the true target, to be taken out with full volley, all Gallowglass men aiming as one. But aim was a relative concept in those days, with those armaments, and any near to Makepeace would perish in the hail. True, the dragoons would be fierce if opening shots spared them, but they were few, and the woman was best left warm.

Manus peered down the lane. Horse dust made a show and the dirt gave a shiver. Back into the trees he went. There his men were covered up in branch and leaf, a forest themselves. All eyes were on him and on the hand he raised—his right.

The hoofbeat grew loud and the buff and pot of the enemy were shuttering between the trunks, winking in the sunlight. With a shout the hand came down.

"Nis!"

The same road and a full gallop brought the three back overland. No need for stealth now, and no means to keep it at a pace so cruel. Spur and crop kept the horses going, and wherever the men called a halt they would die spent to a foam. Sentance had the lead, with a focus that cut the way. The wreck of Jacobs's face wore determination, and Vanderas's own was distraught.

Jacobs's horse gave out first, just atop a rise, as battle came into sight. Tumbling with a cry the beast threw him far, and only a patch of mud kept his neck whole.

Vanderas rode on, after Sentance, and looked to the smoke and noise. Fear rampant in him became something else, raw and primal—the bid of death that underlay it.

Behind them, Jacobs stood and put rifle to shoulder. Barrel and eye found a target, red tartan. A streak as the shot sang past Vanderas, though just, before it struck down a Gallowglass sergeant. Sentance leapt from his mount, odachi drawn, and before feet met earth the whirl took a head, another, a third.

Swung from the horse, Vanderas waded in. His eyes darted over the fallen—many bodies, most in buff coat, sprawled out or crawling and shuddering in the last. Sentance went left, and Vanderas right, into both arms of the pincer, and they never let up. Scrums of Gallowglass men were looking inward until the odachi and the backsword reaped a way. The Scots turned, defended with greatsword and dirk and club, to no use. Sentance moved through, a fluid shadow—feint, duck, turn, nightmarish speed. Only a scream and a mist of blood behind him would show the strike. Vanderas threw even as the backsword lashed and fended. He wore into the thick with a fierce eye that would glance in search. Such distraction had risk—for all his speed Scottish weapons tore his shirt. Jacobs, too, was in the fray now: he had sprinted downslope with basket sword drawn, a smoking pistol in the free hand, then the other of the pair he wore, each thrown aside hot and empty.

The lines broke, and the order of battle fell to madness, man on man in an undifferentiated roar of voice and weapon and the drumming trample of the ground. "Róis!" He never knew who made it, but Vanderas alone could hear the shout. "Róis!" Jacobs saw Calloway not far ahead, and he beat a path. But the lieutenant-general had squared off against a larger man—black beard and a claymore against his thinner blade. Jacobs felt a rush of strength, even as three Scots huddled to him. Each took a wound as the captain stared past, saw the chieftain cut his friend's leg out and pound the claymore down.

"No, no, no," Jacobs cried, beating through the ring of Scots.

Manus Ciotach was already off, hacking through to a wagon toppled for a barricade. Behind it, on a rise in the trees, the general and his dragoons made a stand, shooting into the knot. But something else drew his attention: a lock of red hair shown from a hood. There she was, among the foot soldiers defending Makepeace, the promised woman— covered but not shy with a pistol in hand, then a poignard. This took a Scot at the knuckles, no more than a swipe, and Manus made little note of how he recoiled, screaming and clutching. The scout had not made her out for a ruadh lass—Irishwoman or Scot. Few others could boast that hair. He looked between her and the general, prize that he was. A rider broke that chain of thought—charging in, demilance steady, until Manus rolled aside with a sweep to a leg. The horse cried and fell, bowling through Roundhead and Scot alike.

Jacobs at last made it to his old friend, very much dead and mauled. No time for prayer and rood. The captain brought the grief to the Scots, and soon the witchy bolt struck through his hair went from white to red.

At the wagon the line broke, and Gallowglass fighters raced past a line of foot and up the rise. The dragoons threw carbines aside and took up sabres against the charge. Makepeace drew as well and ran up to the new line of defense, the last.

Confusion—Róis made a stab and lost the poignard to the wound. Caught in breastbone, not deep and not mortal, but the man shrieked as if at a molten scald. Róis tumbled backward, righted herself, and fled for a gap in the trees.

Manus noted it with a relish. The fall had lowered the hood and shown him the face. He looked to the general—the dragoons succumbing, fighting yet like rabid hounds—and back again. The chore was all but done. Mood led him after the ruadh.

The Scots made a surge, tasting the end, and the last of Okey's detachment fell swinging. Makepeace reeled back to the trees to cover his flank. He slashed wildly, too caught up to know his demise, the plans ruined, when Sentance stood up out of the earth. Makepeace woke, feeling the air burn in his chest, and the steel in his deputy's grip flew to the enemy. The general found himself trembling on the ground, overcome, and the Scots shrank from the odachi or what ployed it. Twelve Roundheads had come to the general's defense. Maces took out the Gallowglass men, but for the trouble a few more of the Parliamentary army met death.

A change in fortunes, bought hard—and now the man in black merely stood in place. He looked on from the perimeter he had cut about Makepeace. His flat stare

came back to the general. Makepeace put up a hand—
"Help me up"—but the stare held and he let the hand
fall. Sentance looked out again. Roundheads were falling
yet to enemy soldiers, targets within his range. Unmoved,
studious, he held the ground.

Jacobs had thrown himself into the worst. Shouts
to the foot had reformed a line. The Scots were driven
back in disarray, stumbling over the fallen, and many
of these were their own, Jacobs saw. Those wounds were
unaccounted from that side, and he looked past to see
Vanderas at work. Blood hung in his hair and eyes, and
the shirt was a rag. But for all the fury the man underneath
was unmarked, and Jacobs saw anew what he had seen
years before, on the stone bridge.

The fight went out of him as old light played. He no
longer heard the roar of the day, but another, and from
within. His sword-arm fell limp. Even as a Scottish officer
made a sacrifice, charging in with a gun stock, the trance
was on him. A fellow Roundhead, one of Harry's captains,
shoved him aside to fend the blow, and at last the gaze
broke. Jacobs took up the sword again and rejoined the
fight.

"Róis!" Vanderas heard. The Scots would not relent
but they had thinned enough to see past. More attention
went to the search than to the fight, and it bought him
a gash. He felt the furrow drawn even as he caught a
glimpse of red among the trees.

And of Manus, in pursuit. None expected the burst
of strength, him least of all. In truth he ran through the
Scots amassing to him, knocking arms aside like pins.

A fresh wound to his ribcage went unnoticed, and the Scots were too engrossed in Jacobs's push to give chase. A vault over the dead piled three men deep. About the windrows a rich pond stood. The last hazes of gunsmoke cleared, and above the trees Vanderas saw the ramshackle eaves and rooftop of a horse mill.

Róis saw the derelict, too, with hopes of a hiding place. But next she saw the big man on her heels. Into the building she went, and double fast. There she took a place behind the millstone, space narrow enough to serve. She waited, waited—what lay in store ran through her mind. Hostilities had grown faint, and not just for the distance.

Manus heard the wane, too, and took it for a rout. Crows for victory were near, and the lads would begin to spoil on the enemy, dead or alive. There were better choices. He chuckled and ducked below a lintel. Welcome dark, private time.

Come out of the trees, Vanderas shied the last knife from the belt. Had the arm been unwounded the chieftain would have fallen. But the try fell short, unheard in the weeds, and Vanderas ran anew.

Knitting hook in hand, Róis stood ready. Manus saw her in the nook where straw lay on the ground. She had not bothered to hide. Perhaps they were of a like mind here. But then he made out the needle in the dim light and he laughed aloud.

In response the ruadh gave a smirk—wicked, cold, and sure. Strange enough to stop the laughter, but not the motive. Manus made a lunge, and it bought his cheek a wee scratch. He stepped back, touching at the bloodless smite and chiding her. A second laugh was near but his throat had already caught and closed.

Vanderas ran in. He had taken up the stiletto on the run and now he threw it once again. Clumsy for him, but close, and with a thump a shoulder was spitted.

The Scot seemed not to react at all. He took a step back, another. There a patch of light showed Vanderas the face—swollen, strangling, black as the beard. The mouth let out no scream, nor so much as a squeak of air. Foam was bubbling upon the lip, and the eyes rolled white. As Vanderas watched the bloat closed them altogether, and the first scratch split open to bone.

Róis had stepped out to watch the struggle. A cruel look was on her—comeuppance, a tight smile. The Scot fell to his knees, clutching at her skirts.

"End it or don't," she said. "The fool's dead already."

Done, with a thrust to the nape that broke the spine. Battle had fallen no less still than did the chieftain, though the flesh continued to purple and swell. Vanderas looked to her. He read the sneer and saw the hook in hand. The thought showed—connecting the knitting tool to that agony, that blossoming wound—but he dropped the backsword, stepped up, and gently took her in his arms.

Surprise to both, but most of all to Róis. The clinch went unreturned at first, but the spite broke on her face, if only to surprise. No strong welcome, but she did hold the stinger out to let it fall away. The harmless hand went to his shoulder. She closed her eyes, took a breath, and felt a little more humanity return.

Keeping close, he broke the hold. A fluster was on him. None of the arrogance was shown, only a boyishness, strangely worn on a man near to middle age. But the relief in his eyes was no less clear when he found the nerve to glance up to her.

"You're trembling," she said, puzzled again.

"Jo havia—havia pensat—"

With a touch to his face, "Joaquim, don't be ridiculous."

They left sight of the miseries behind. From her skirts she tore out a strip for his bleeding arm. There were no more sounds of a fight past the trees, save two shots that might have been a signal. The thought nagged at her—how this new turn could be put to use, and to her favor—but she held it back. A better nature was long starved in her breast, and now it came to her defense, fed in spite of everything.

No signal, the gunshots. Battle had grown sparse, casualties strewn about dead and wounded, but a few Scots had kept the dander up. Jacobs was picking off the last fuss. Matchlit guns had been dropped for the charge, and at the verges a few were smoking yet and loaded. Jacobs took one up and brought a man down, another, and another, though not the one he had been aiming for. Crude gunsmithing—he made a face and threw the barrel aside. He found no need to recharge his own—the shots had spooked the last of the enemy, who ran for the trees, up the road, anywhere else.

Danger past, Jacobs watched himself fall to knees. The will had gone, a strength borrowed since the day before.

Hand set to dirt, a dry sob of breath. He looked about. Much wreckage, man and cart and horse, but many of the Roundheads were intact. Seeing as much, and no enemy yet close, the shrunken ranks began to cheer.

Makepeace had come down from the rise, and Sentance remained behind, looking on. Men who could yet walk began to converge, and the general stepped among them. The cheer was taken up again, fiercely loud. Those on the ground joined in, even for their injuries, some mortal, and Jacobs, too, once he had a mind to stand. It felt good on his face, that smile and cry, and he turned now to the wounded.

Vanderas and Róis came out from the trees. His gait was steady but she had an arm to his waist. A strip had been applied to his ribs, where it slid, grown heavy and wet. And the Roundheads turned to see him and the blood drawn, a man brightly hurt in defense of their lives. Half had watched him sweep the enemy—no less a spectacle than the wrath in gospel. As Jacobs watched the cheer go up again—welcome—he felt relief fade. And by the time the general had gone up to Vanderas's side, hand to his shoulder to lead the thanks, the smile had died altogether.

Warm salutes—and in reply a nonplussed look. Vanderas had been happier at sight of Róis than he was for any cheer, and now she stood off so he could take a place among the English. But she did not stray far, and she looked past, to the rise. There Sentance stood alone—far enough that she could not see the features of his face and where it looked, but she felt the gaze light upon her all the same.

\* \* \*

Peasants had a way of showing up, however bare of croft or field the country march had been. And here they were by eventide, dozens pulled from empty miles on the scent of loot. The Scottish dead were fair salvage, and shabby men and women searched among them with torch and lamp. Others had gone to the Roundhead camp, not far at all, for an actual wage. There had been tents to raise, fires to light, water to heat up. Potted meat was cooking on the spit, and the mood had gone sour as soldiers began to tend the hurt. Men were dying yet and once fever set in they would continue to die for days to come. Those succumbed in the moment of battle had been sewn into duck and blanket and laid in rows on high ground, awaiting rites. Menial work dug the holes, two yards long for each man, two deep. Creeds among that army did not take to High Anglican, but a vicar in surplice walked from shroud to shroud with readings from the Book of Common Prayer, for he was all they had.

Captain Jacobs knelt at the end of a row. Even as the priest drew close he spoke to the veteran in the womb of cloth, and he held a candle. The wick swung a flame to the quiet of his voice. Goodbyes said, Jacobs walked away. Without a thought he let the candle drop, and the wick snuffed before wax began to gel on the ground.

*　*　*

Where no quarterings were available Róis had a tent to herself, one crafted especially for her use. The canvas was unusually heavy and well insulated. Sound came through only faintly, and the strange odors could not waft out. Her work took secrecy, true, but this was just as much for caution. Much of what she made was dangerous even to a casual nose. When she was alone there with the apothecary jars, an alembic, a pestle, and other tools she wore a special visard. Tubes would redirect her breathing to the back, and there a sachet of herbs and chrism made a filter. So masked, she would think about mutterings caught outside, told at her back. "Romish witch" was a favorite. In its way it was even said fair.

But she was not alone that night, nor at that work. Vanderas had a snore on her cot, shirtless, with a line of stitches on his ribs. That darning would leave a wondrous scar, and not the first, she saw. His back carried nine pits. A cloth wiped the needle clean, or a corner of it not already left rich. "Nursemaid again, by God," Róis said, but in Irish, and without complaint. Her expression was tired but no longer in a scowl for the task—almost tender, in truth, as she looked to him before she remembered herself and reapplied the frown.

On went a blanket, and he never woke. Róis found herself looking on from the portable chair at the work table, yarns in hand once more. She looked down to the absent knitting, the gauges of the crochet hooks. No purl, knit, or stitch to it of any kind. She had shown real craft once, and she could fashion small articles of clothes and large without trouble if she had a mind to. The present snarl was an idle thing—ugly, spendthrift, no use at all—and she threw it aside and put the hooks away.

Makepeace was yet in conference with the surviving captains, and at the appointed time she waited outside the command tent. "Give out the stores of brandy," the general was saying. "Every last cask. I'll address the men tomorrow after Wooldridge arrives. Likely what remains will disband and be absorbed." A scout with sealed letters came out and made for a horse without a glance to her. "The general is coming from the north," Makepeace went on. "He'll take word overnight. Whatever Scots remain will covet our animals and food, any they can take. Let's make sure they go hungry on their own two feet."

The captains filed out. None saw Róis—part of what went unspoken in camp. Sentance had a corner once again, and he was what she herself knew not to see. Makepeace was at a trestle desk. Before it a stool had been set, and so she knew where to go. She waited through his stare.

"Tomorrow night," he said at last. "I needn't stress how well it resemble nature. Vanderas has taken to you, has he not?"

She looked up in a snap. "Englishman, that's no concern of yours." The cold anger was a surprise to both. But Róis realized what she had said, the predicament, and the glare broke off.

The general's smile was faint and slow in coming. "Sometimes I forget which is a matter of profession.

Good night." Once she was gone, put to her use again, Makepeace spoke to the desk before him. "Loyalties: so rarely all they seem."

"Ambitions made a fool of you. Do as need be."

"Strange—you were misled as well. I never thought I'd say the like."

"That, too, is no concern of yours."

Róis did not know she would lie beside him until she had. Once she settled in, a corner of the blanket crept to her shoulder, and she could not say that she had drawn it up, only that the warmth was good. The snore had quit but Vanderas had not moved. She was careful of the stitches even as she puzzled at her own mind. Such a cheap notion— to want being wanted—and when her life was at stake, mere foolishness. But she could not bear it, her part in these subterfuges, not for the moment. She had meant to scheme there in the camp chair—how to use one man against another, whatever came of the one grown fond of her. But sight of the rogue brought to her cot, facing away, lain on a side—trusting—left too bitter a taste, and she stood up from the slouching watch. The thought of poison was more a comfort, and the work more honest. A night's sleep would recruit her, and she would get to brewing, with little choice. No more ruses, not where the decision was hers to make. His affections were silly, puppyish, founded in nothing, and that was all the more reason to leave them be. She let out a breath.

The voice was sudden but gentle. "Envenenador," he said in his native tongue, faced yet away. "Poisoner, I mean. What brought you to it?"

"Marriage."

He did not stir. Perhaps the ache kept him in place. She found her hand on his waist, considered pulling it away, let it rest.

"Does it surprise you," she asked, "that he'd use such foul tricks?"

"The general? He's, how to put it, a man of ideas. Never mind him—marriage, you said. Your husband? He was the first?"

"But not soon enough."

"He was cruel to you."

Róis might have shed a tear once, but the wound was dry now, and deep set—as much a part of her as any bone. "Not to me alone. In all of nature there's venom. One need only learn how to draw it out, how to keep it."

"You found a way then—a means, I should say—in going free. And as a widow left without any other trade, you plied the trade you could."

"Harlotry aside." Róis was surprised by, even wary of, how easily she spoke. Perhaps it was for whom she told, or what—this man who had done worse than she, yet seemed to know regret. "Other wives, other mothers. Or lasses who would be shamed. Before the mistake they made quickened in them. Near when the rebellion started I was caught. Rather than hang I did as those in charge bade me to. A wife's last resort, a daughter's—it became a governor's first. Men see an end better than they ever see a method. Say what you like about me afore then, what I did, but right or wrong it felt necessary. Good might come of it, or better. I lost that reason, that place in things, so I did. And worse, I came to the attention of mister Sentance."

Vanderas said nothing, but she felt him tense.

"Aye, he was there, Joaquim. Behind another of your men of ideas."

"Sentance—he brought you here from Irlanda?"

"There I'm an outlaw. No, I was in Wales then, in the countryside, and back to a wives' business. Makepeace has agents. He led spies in the last war, and he still does, from his own belt poke. I hadn't known Sentance's part before they brought me to the man in charge and I saw just who stood behind. I knew better than to ken him."

"Know? He's familiar to me as well, but I can't say how. I'd remember a hand so quick, even from the haze. It was not from a duel, I can say that. One of us would be dead. Yet there's something—at Clitheroe, what he did there, that silent work. It almost frightened me."

"Almost," she said drowsily.

"He's got you spooked." His hand went back to hers, where it lay on his waist. "You'd make him out for the devil."

"Here a devil would go to waste." Said of things seen firsthand, but from the verge of sleep.

Vanderas took a moment to gather up the courage. The words were halt. "Róis. I've never—I haven't—only of late—." His mouth was wry and he let out a breath. "I have no use for kind thoughts. I don't know what to say. I've been a different man."

A snore was the answer. It left a tickle on his ear, soft and warm, and he held a laugh that might have rung strange to him, had he let it out. In all of nature, there is venom, she had said. Perhaps she was wrong, on that at least. Laughter could be innocent. As might joy. His eyes fell shut, grown weighty on the skin of the tent.

Scouts had the lead as Wooldridge rode in the next morning, and hard. Along the tents there were honors paid, but weary, much unlike the recent pomp. But the ranks did come out for him: silent, bandaged men whose friends were dying yet all about them. The general gave inspection without breaking pace—every show of concern.

Jacobs met him at the command tent. A crisp salute, a dismount, and a hand to a shoulder as Wooldridge said, "You're unhurt, praise."

"Not all went as planned. But we did get to kill a lot of Scots."

"You rode back? And in time to give aid. How ever did you make it?"

This would go unanswered, for Makepeace had come out. Careworn, underslept, but otherwise he was regimental, with clean clothes and a salute. The generals looked to each other, communicating without a word before the embrace. And in that close hold neither man could read the flatness of an eye.

Scriveners had been brought in, a pair, and they made work on dispatches and orders at the usual camp table. On another, just beside, salt pork had been laid out with cheeses and rusk and a pair of empty goblets. Here Makepeace and Wooldridge sat, with Sentance and Jacobs behind.

"I'm loath to see your regiments diminished," Wooldridge said to Makepeace. "Or further so, alas."

"That the men have provision is all that matters. I'll pay out the last of the chest before I head south."

"Better you wait. A Covenanter is a slippery ally at best. There's hardly enough mettle up there to hold back the engager faction. And now Gordon men—as you saw. For all we know Montrose will be turning up again. A push will come from the north—the last, and soon. What you met, Stephan, it was but a foretaste."

"There are few hands left to push back."

Sentance looked to Jacobs, and sharply. The captain had been studying the unwrapped face—subtly, he had thought. With disregard he looked past, away again.

"I can't have it," Wooldridge was saying. "Parliament's finest young commander, returned to the City without a host? You've been put up as my alternate, after all. Papers I sign here and now can affirm the chain of command—my own regiments and all of the Northern Association. No delays from the War Commission. No vetting, no oil. We need you out here—and the war won't last. The only question is how hard it winds down for the men left on watch."

Makepeace gave every appearance of thought. At last he smiled. "Keep me out of chambers for another month? Well, I do hate all the speechifying."

"As befits a man of action." The general raised a hand to the scribes. "A copy to be posted up north, and one for the lieutenant-general. The order will go out ahead of me, and right away. Excellent, Stephan. A glass, if you please—to our renewal."

"Glass is rare stuff out here, save for broken shards. These tinker's cups will serve. By all means, though— let's drink."

Some were dry, others wet, and Róis had a use for each— especially those meant for food or drink. The present task made use of a hermetic vase to catch the flowers of a draught. This swelter had gone to the retort, and to further heat—six candles in a stove. Potash in, the result fell out like grains of salt—grains that vanished into drink, and without taste or nose. With the counteragent it was much the same. Romish witch, she thought again, breathing through the deeps of her visard.

Directed outside the canvas, her new friend paced nearby, working off stiffness and a limp. From stitches to stitches—pains that shot from the thread drawn tight. Aside from one bad day years back, and those grave, Vanderas had never taken wounds. He thought of the slowness as a rust. Only use could mend him faster, use or drink, and one of these he forbid himself.

Not the Roundheads, though—officer's stores had been given out. Beers became the bread, and even poor Harold Calloway's store of whisky went into service. A quiet tippling, however—partly in respect for the visiting general, and partly in that for the dead. There were laughs, though, a lightening of the mood.

Vanderas heard Jacobs's approach—could not but—but his mind was no less busy than his tender step. The captain stopped short and awaited an eye, measuring words. "I thank you for aiding us yesterday," he said. "You saved many of my friends' lives—a hero's work. Yet I can't forget what you've done and how we came to meet. This is yours." Jacobs touched the eyepatch. "I was on the bridge at Gaddis."

"Where?"

The air grew sour, and nothing moved. But as Jacobs broke the stare and made to leave—a fast turn—Vanderas spoke again. "I'm sorry, Captain."

"Sorry? Regret what you can't recall?"

"That I don't. You'll strike from the back, I'll gamble, and it would have gone easier if I had. But whatever it was you met on a bridge at Gaddis, that's here still."

No mockery, no dare, only a plainspoken truth.

Jacobs weighed it. "I would never blindside a man," he said. "Any man." The command tent was immediately beside, and once the captain cleared the view it seemed that Sentance had stepped out as well. He had been watching the exchange.

Vanderas stepped up. A trained eye would have seen that he did so just out of range. "Tell me about the sword, would you?"

Sentance lowered the scarf. There was no hesitation in the draw—this underhand, and gentle. The odachi went high and plumb like a monstrance.

"That's a beauty," Vanderas said. He made no reach, drew no closer. "Foreign, like mine, and who could say from where. Mine was spoils. What of yours?"

"No," Sentance said.

"No? No is no answer."

"No is the only answer."

Sentance took a sidestep, and Vanderas went tense. But the move was only meant to clear the way. Róis had come out of her tent, in the lace bodice of a serving wench. Her eyes were down, studiously so, with no acknowledgment to either man. In the crook of an arm she carried a basket with fruit and a clay decanter full of wine.

Vanderas said nothing, put on no face, but his eyes sought the basket. And on that glance, slight though it was, Sentance said, "She told you."

"What?"

"Such is intimacy. Hardly a surprise."

"I don't know what you—"

"She knew the value of caution but let you near. You're the only man she's welcomed so in spite of all you've done. No matter. She's struck a bargain."

Horror had mounted—hid less well on every breath—to an outright chill. Vanderas took a step closer—fair reach for either man, though only one had a weapon out. "Harm her, Sentance, speak ill of her, and you answer to me. It misled you, our spat last week, when I was shaking sick. You'd answer, do you hear?"

"I'd answer," Sentance said. A slow push returned the odachi to the sheath.

"A wench, among an army? Now why ever didn't I think of that?"

The cup was filled, and Róis stepped away from Wooldridghe. She busied herself to the other side, where the selfsame wine went into the other cup.

"There are advantages," Makepeace said. Next she offered him the fruit in the basket, and a bruised pear was the choice. Prime though it was, Wooldridge had declined the other. Produce was rare in the field, and Makepeace wolfed it down. Juice ran as he picked up a linen to mop his face. "Fruit—it sharps all flavors."

Wooldridge said, "A drink with you, sir." Both men stood from the dinner table to raise a cup. "The fallen."

"Hear, hear," Makepeace said. "Well may they rest."

Wine returned to table with a clap, what little went undrained. When the generals had seated themselves once more, Wooldridge said, "Stephan, I regret my role in this. Such an ambush—the intelligence on Clitheroe had to have been part of a plan. Even to the time of day, they were ready for you. It's obvious, is it not?"

"It is."

"Spies—the prospect was not lost on us, not at all," Wooldridge said. "But it seems precaution came up short. The two of us both know a thing or two about about the art. I should have known a ruse. Had I suspected …" Wooldridge trailed off on a throat gone dry. He glanced about for the wench, the bottle.

"Trades for kin and country are no handsome buy. Besides, your hearsay was accurate."

"Where'd she get to? Accurate, you said?"

Makepeace rose. He picked up his chair by the back and brought it close to Wooldridge. Along the way he took up a second decanter. Once seated for the intimate talk, he pulled the stopper, filled the cup. "Accurate, yes. Accurate in its ends." Straight from the mouth of the jar he took his own swallow.

"What do you suspect?"

"I suspect nothing: I know. When Sentance and his party reached the fort, it was nearly empty. Desert a post—that's a move made only in certitude."

"They met up with the Scots, yes, the men stationed there." The general took a good swallow.

"And the Scots knew our road. Little mystery—few routes close on that valley, and even fewer that could march a host. But it is as you said. A garrison, whose sole duty is to hold fast and keep watch, that goes out and hides—it tells the tale—"

"Of course."

"—but not the full. They had scouts. So they knew where the larger force was camped, and with their very position in mind. Your horse and foot, your long guns, were no less sure to move. Yet out they went. They must have known you'd stay put."

The suspicion had already begun to show. "What do you suggest?"

"I suggest nothing: I state. This is a time of upheaval, and kingless we hardly know how to rule. Parliament's a babel—a shout that never ends. We hear fine points of religion and haggles over a bill of goods. England is exposed. A man of conscience could hardly let that go on. To protect the realm, he would do anything."

The general had trouble finding his voice, and it came hoarse. "Stephan, you'd call me a judas?"

"Cliff, I was speaking of myself."

Wooldridge rose, or tried, but cleared no further than a foot before he came down hard to the seat. Now the voice was gone, and the color in the face went with it. A hand overturned the cup. What dregs were the bottom rolled out before it.

Makepeace kept a gentle tone, and the regret was sincere. "You breath is still, you'll find. But you can hear me yet. We both drank it. The pear I ate, second best, that was what hid the cure. Be assured, friend—she made it painless." Wooldridge's eyes found different ends of the tent, and the pupils shrank to points. Makepeace set a hand to his forearm. "I know it wasn't you. No more than this is me. The rank, the burdens, these are the devil. There was no malice on either part—no betrayal except to a rout down in London. No, all this was just a question of who stood against them, who brought the squabbles to a close—and of who best."

Throes took Wooldridge from his seat, and the chair fell with him.

Not without tears. Murder was no less sad for the need. Makepeace gathered his thoughts. Rome was the lesson—not the papacy, but the older Rome, what the Latin city had been long before that corrupt regime. So history told it: once rid of kings, fortunes had been won, and the republic became a mercantile power. But its fame had soared highest later, under a soldier, a conquering general. In time kings forgot what bought their ease, cossets that they were, but no man at arms ever could. So Gaius Octavian had become August, first in laurels, and of many. A long peace—the wars like those under the republic were done with for three hundred years.

Makepeace would have told his mentor, why not skip a step? He would have vowed that England would outlast the times. More, it would thrive, and in good tutelage. The land and the people did not need a kingdom, but a protectorate.

Said or not, what was sworn had already been taken to heart. Wooldridge wore a voided look as the simmer of life stole away—the face of sincerity itself.

All a cruel necessity—one more rival gone. Now only the grandee remained. Not Black Tom—a fair man and a fine soldier, but without the bottom for rule. No, the other, he with his name already told—most recently in Wales, and busy in Preston. A man of reach and appetite, much used to seeing his will done.

Wept out, Makepeace put on a face for the tent flap. "A physician! Quickly!"

\* \* \*

Róis heard the cry from the table where she sat, thick though the canopy was. Any devices in the tent had been broken down and stowed away, to beds of straw in boxes under latch and key. But the general's voice, inevitable though it was, made her pause. Looking out from the tent flap would have made for a better ruse, but she had no heart to stand and take further part. She had asked a question days before but knew the answer well enough herself. No joy—a thankless busywork. It had not always been so. Grim though the role had gone, some men deserved a quench. Few of the women who had come to her, often with a closed eye and a bloody mouth, did so with any relish. Sorry business, but necessary. And so it had been with the younger ones, come to rid before the show, with no choices but the worse. The bastard who had followed her to the millstone, slavering like a hound—he had met his deserts. Just, nothing short of just, and nothing to shame her.

Yet here she was—without the heart to stand, take further part in the whole foul ruck. Outside the commotion rose—footfall, a shout.

And in came Vanderas, without ask or leave. He stood and waited. She did not turn—the stare remained on the hands set on the tabletop—and he said, "We must flee. Tonight."

"You're being daft again."

"It's not safe. You're not safe here."

90

"I never was."

"I'll take you. I'll protect you. I love you."

A moment went. But there was no unsaying so dull a thing. Her gaze was firm in front of her, though the focus was no longer on the hands. "You've never known the like," she said at last.

"I know I haven't."

If briefly, this won—fool or not, he meant it. Looking like an older self, she gave him the attention he sought. "The things we've done," she said. "This camp—it's but a foretaste. What's love here? Spittle in a fire. Another knot in hand. Nothing for nobody. A waste."

He knelt before her, and the concern showed like an ache. "Put these men behind you. What can Makepeace do? Once we're far, lost to him, he'll see we're no threat. That hound of his, he'll call him off. Get on with his wickedness."

"Of his." She shook her head. "You're blind, Joaquim. Blind. Watch them, and watch close. Always that whisper to the ear. What do you think is said?" He made to answer but she raised a hand. "In Ireland he did the same. The name was different, but nothing else. Whispering … always the whisper, always at a well-placed ear. In the revolt I met a man for hire, much like yourself. A Dutch mercenary, half thief and all business. He remembered Sentance too, so he told me. From years past, and by yet another name. And the ear he had then was the Prince of Orange."

Vanderas seemed to weigh it, though not without a doubt. "Dutch independence. He gets around. But that would make him old—far older than he seems."

"Oh yes. And seeming is all there is with him. The Hollander, the man at arms, I said he was much like you, but not so full in gifts. He himself was showing the wear of age. And he shared that tale of his youth. Not long after he was found in a privy hole. When they hauled him out on a rope, dripping shit and offal, his head hung backward like a cowl. The man you call Sentance, he didn't have me brought just for my work, but it's how I buy my time. Poison is my life."

Vanderas put a hand to her knee. She allowed it. "What else—what do you know of him besides?"

"More than I'll tell, yet nothing—nothing. For all the trouble he gets to there's little to the man himself—less than in that whisper. None see him off guard. He doesn't sleep, or eat, drink, not that any witness. Think on that. He must. But he keeps no tent—he's never part of where he visits. What moves him? What could a man want if not love, ease, a place in things? What does he say to that ear?"

The fear had only built, and with it the resolve. Vanderas leaned in. "I can't let you stay, Róis. I won't let you."

"And what's your stake in it? You don't even know the name I was born to. Róis Nimhiúil, that's apt enough, though. It means venom—"

"I don't care what it means."

"You don't know me. You don't know me at all."

"Needs be I'll take you off by force."

"Aye, Joaquim—and there's all you've known of womenfolk."

The effect was more than she had meant. The hand fell away, and he looked to it and to other times, with remorse. No less hurt than if she had dealt out a blow—in truth worse. And she regretted the words, true though they doubtless were. Look at us, she said to herself. Us both—what we've done, what we are for it.

She reached to his chin, raised his eye to hers. No apology, no fault, but a tender look. He seemed a boy to her, strangely callow for a life so ruthless, so full of trespass, and halfway done. Love—absurd, and not less for such a man. But the gaze held, and the reluctance fell. In mind she said, as if to him, Name it as you like, this welcome of me, and he seemed to hear. She slid from the chair to her own knees, cupping his face and the nape of his neck. Her ambitions were on the brushed patch of dirt—good enough for a rut—but hands to shoulders he stopped her. They rose for the cot, where a passion built. They tore the clothes away, stripping bare, with her atop. In the straddle she led him with a hand. Abandoned to each other they no longer heard the sounds that built just outside the tent, gruesome though they were.

"Make way! Let me through!"

Jacobs broke through the muttering press of soldiers. Wooldridge's elite dragoons held them back with hard face and gunstock, and he nearest the tent flaps sidled for the captain. Inside Jacobs found four live men—Makepeace, Sentance, the priest, and the camp surgeon—and beneath a saddle blanket, yet another.

"No God no!"

The captain fell to knees beside the general supine on the floor. In respect for the grief all but Sentance turned away. Jacobs took up the makeshift pall to see the face, to confirm it, and then from the hand, to take a hold.

And abruptly his sob caught in his mouth, and he gave a pointed stare.

To Sentance's own. Sentance had no vantage on the body itself, laid out as it was behind the table, but he saw Jacobs's face: the glance toward the feet, the frown, the suspicion. But the captain looked to no one, least to Sentance, and he covered up the general once again. A quick rise and a brisk pace took him from the tent. Men could be heard asking after him, to no answer.

"Send in four of the guard," Makepeace shouted, and in came dragoons. "A stretcher," he said. "The quartermaster has a tent to spare. Have it raised, then come back and take him there." He turned to the surgeon. "Better he be received down in London. Perhaps a balm would serve, before he's placed into the bier ... wait."

The guards had gone, and the priest, and now Makepeace waved the surgeon out. Sentance had knelt to the corpse. He turned back the wool for a close study. Nothing seemed to linger in his attention. Down came the muffler, and he stood from the crouch and stepped quite close to Makepeace.

"Before the cry you made inspection, did you not?"

The general hesitated—to a backhand blow, and strong. Makepeace caught the floor, and his terror at the rebuke, more, was as open as his mouth.

"A note," Sentance said, looming over. "Might there have been a note?"

"No. Impossible. He was already dying—gone stiff."

The contempt—the icy vehemence—wholly changed the face that wore it. Sentance hunkered down, and Makepeace dared no move.

"So. You spoke—for vanity your part shown to the man you betrayed. And he took every word to heart."

Up went the scarf, and Sentance was gone.

The hurry, the hand to the scabbard beneath his cloak, went unseen by any in the tent. Two men were on the floor, one yet alive. He rose and composed himself, but the fright haunted him and would for hours yet, until the glimpse he had caught became deniable, something from a nightmare. Only when dragoons came back for the unhappy task did he seem the man in charge once more.

Pointing—that hand, not yet cold, had been pointing. There was no mistaking such a gesture. The finger had pointed at nothing, to a blameless corner of the tent. But a closer look had shown the captain more—the ruby stain there on the fingertip.

Roundheads began to mourn as word spread, and Jacobs walked among them with no action yet in mind, no destination. His thought raced well ahead, with a dread he could not shake. Wandering the rows, with the night air gone wet again—not quite a drizzle, nor a fog, but a cloud come down to creep among them.

And Sentance roamed the lanes, too, with an eye for Jacobs. Quite by chance the two missed each other, and just as Jacobs doubled back toward the command tent, a man of the same build and dress redirected Sentance and led him astray.

Jacobs passed the quartermaster's tent, and seeing a jug laid out among the rations took it up without breaking stride. No drink had—he pulled a glove and poured out a trickle. The fingertip took the stain, the selfsame ruby stain. He had known it would, though the meaning was not yet apparent. The jug fell, and he meandered on. By then Sentance had seen his mistake and had doubled back, at a pace no less urgent.

Near the command tent Roundheads had begun to disperse, many at a hobble—even those not game from injury. Some followed the dragoons and their load, but most were headed off for whatever drink remained in camp. From opposite ends Jacobs and Sentance came into the row. And both stopped short when Vanderas took a step partway out from the flaps of Róis's tent.

Jacobs watched him, and Sentance watched Jacobs. Róis herself was just inside. She and the mercenary stood close, face to face—a faltering smile and a kiss that held. Not just intimate, happy, but—as Jacobs saw it—conspiratorial.

The scowl grew, along with a flush. He reached to a pistol at his waist. But Róis pulled Vanderas back inside, and the tent flaps closed. The captain let his hand fall, and he turned, walking hard.

Before the turn, the angry paces, the light in the unmaimed eye had shown the hostility, an urge that could only build. And Sentace had made full note of it. A step back just behind a tent peg—the black of cloak and scarf hid him well.

Makepeace was on the cot in a dark of his own, and camp had gone quiet. A shape stood at the entry to the tent.

"He'll try," the general said. "He's a deeply moral man. Wooldridge told him nothing, I don't doubt. Jacobs simply wouldn't abide the tricks. To let so fine an officer dash himself, go to court martial ... worse still, Róis. And Vanderas. Up close Jacobs is no danger. But Vanderas can only leave him dead. The men will turn again, self-defense or not. He'll slay a few dozen, flee, and take our Irishwoman along. Two assets lost."

"Better two than all else," the whisper.

"Perhaps we should let them. If Jacobs shares what he suspects, the men will take them for fugitives—fleeing the crime. There's use in that."

"She's a detail not yet settled. If not for the work in store—if not for the problem of Oliver Cromwell—that loose end would have been made fast long ago."

Makepeace might have gone to sleep already, for the whisper came in dreams no less often than it spoke aloud. Whenever sleep began, it passed without fit. Come morning the general found against all expectation that he had rested well.

* * *

Jacobs did not, and camp was struck early for the march. Once the files were moving north—much reduced, and slow—he kept his mount beneath a trot. The cumber was like a second rider, and he a second horse. Jacobs held the rear, along with an honor guard of six dragoons and a covered wagon serving for a hearse. Two hundred and fifty miles awaited those rims and spokes, much of it on indifferent road, and by the time they met city cobblestones what was left of the man in the crate would be quite unlike the man himself. Best the lid stay shut, and memory suffice.

The first leg was westward, to avoid a worse slog through the fells. Silent, haggard, Jacobs stared ahead, gun at right shoulder. All there were wary of stragglers, hidden in the countryside with a desperation that could only have grown. All of them kept armaments near and primed. But the captain was not looking out among the copses or rocks, but to the head of the line, where Vanderas and the Irishwoman rode. They did not do so quite abreast, and they only snuck glances to one another. Without design Jacobs took the strap from his shoulder and laid the barrel across the saddlehorns, with the right hand tickling at the trigger loop.

The files came to a fork in the road. Here the course led north, to the fallen general's cantonment, the sole country house for miles. The march bent, but when the wagon and honor guard came up, they split off. Jacobs pulled the bridle. In the halt the horse gave a nod. The coterie had grown no less small than the host before a snap of reins got her on course again, gladly at a canter, then a gallop, to close the distance.

Daylight did not bring the foot and horse to the destination, so they made a bivouac on the road pan itself. Not many fires were lit for the evening, save for the comfort of the gravely wounded, and supper was tack and beer and a hard cheese with mold cut free. Even for a Lancashire summer, the day had grown cold. Most men went straight to the depths of their blankets to catch up the heat of breath, be damned to the stink.

A brake of trees told a creek, and Róis took out a pair of wooden pails. With nonchalance Vanderas had gone to a trunk, and there he cleaned his backsword and whatever throwing knives he had managed to recover from the slain. The was no gesture—a faint smile on her turn back toward the camp—and he waited a good minute before he rose and followed.

Jacobs took a moment of his own, watching on the sly, before he was on his feet. He went to a spot a hundred yards up from where they had gone into the undergrowth. Upstream, he gathered—better to mask his approach.

The creek obliged, with a rill through a bed of clacking gravel. As he moved beneath its limb a red squirrel gave a plaint. The floor was thick and shrubby, and Jacobs could not see far ahead. First he made out buckets, cast aside near the watercourse. A stone's throw from there the traitors were underneath a wool, all their clothes in a sloppy shuck. The backsword and knives were close in reach. Only affections, as yet, but with a heat that grew.

"Ay, it's goddam freezing out here," Jacobs heard the Irishwoman say. Venery was no surprise—only natural that harlot and scoundrel should disport themselves. And once motions had begun, be so vocal about it, too.

The rifle was ready. It never went unloaded save for cleaning and for rite. He touched his thumb to the jaw screw on the lock, drew it to the hammer catch.

That sparest click raised a head—Vanderas, from beneath the fabric.

Jacobs went still. He did not duck. With so thick a cover, and no sunlight behind or in front, movement would be the giveaway. So faint a noise, to be heard by that ear—the captain feared the pounding of his heart.

Slender hands came up to guide the face back down. Once the lust was in full again, Jacobs took aim. Vanderas's head was in his sights. For such a marksman, a simple shot—he could land it with the patch moved to the remaining eye.

Later, as Vanderas and Róis got dressed in the twilight, he listened to them speak but could not make out words. He had lain still, to an ache.

The Irishwoman said, "You truly think there's a chance we could be done of this? Should we, come what may, I'll never cook so for men again."

Done of this—that was all that Jacobs heard. And Vanderas said nothing, only hid a simper.

"Not this way," he said to himself once they were gone, just as he had done in mind on drawing the bead. "Like a thief." But he only felt a coward. Better friends to Calloway and Wooldridge would never scruple a shot.

He stood, and he saw the pails left behind—ploy that they were, empty. Kicks sent them to the water, vicious kicks, yet they landed upright, to a float. Current bore them along, scraping rock, and whether they made the valley before they foundered—and then the sea—is small conjecture.

Where the decimated army washed up was a much surer thing: along the River Lune. There a member of the Jacobean gentry had bought grounds. A mile off was a span of gritstone put up three centuries before, and without it there never would have been a house or a need for a garrison. The remainder of Makepeace's foot and horse went over it at a slow pinch, with a thicket of barricades cleared back on sight of their approach. The bridge guard, some three hundred men, stood in two rigid rows as their comrades shambled through. The salutes were no less crisp, and any shock or horror at the injuries was kept in check. As Jacobs set foot on the bridge, last in the march, that other bridge sprang to mind. The weathered rail scraped beneath his hand—an ashlar build much the same, more lichen shown than rock. He looked ahead to where Vanderas and the harlot rode, but they were lost in the number. The bridge guard knew him—were glad to see the adjutant alive and well—but he gave little more than a nod. Once he was past they reassembled the defenses.

The country house was not old, in truth. The first war saw its master vanish, and since then it had gone into only minor disrepair. In effect Wooldridge's forces had commandeered it from nobody. The house sat atop a low hill just aside the river course, and the Roundheads had set to digging up the gardens. The redoubt set up was a formidable defense—circle within circle of earthworks and palisades with multiple emplacements for cannon and small arms. The approach was a winding affair, much like the rocky waterway it sat beside. The river landing was secure, with sheer bedrock on either side nearer to the house. Storehouses were kept here, with oilcloth to keep out the damps, and north and south of the dock wooden ramparts stood above moatlike inlets. No rider could approach there, nor infantry without a swim, and gunfire from the walkways would keep them honest.

Outside the redoubt was a sprawling camp, full of tents, wagons, makeshift stables for horse and swine, gun racks, blacksmiths, farriers, quartermasters, sutlers, a few drudging peasants, and thousands of well-armed Roundheads. Smoke rose from fires, and the near woodland was halfway shorn to stumps to keep them in fuel.

Makepeace had gone to the head of the files, and there he sat, upright and in a stern dignity as they neared the lane that had cleared. Soldiers along the way were at faultless presentation, and hats came off to receive the new commander. The men who walked behind Makepeace and Sentance also straightened their backs, even those who bore along with a crutch or a splinted arm.

Wooldridge's men could only warm to the valor. Cries came from the ranks: "Welcome, lads!" "Well done of Lancaster!" And only built, to a general cheer. "All hail General Makepeace!" "Godspeed you, general!" Spreading out, grown to a roar—within moments the downbeat air was wholly renewed and proud.

Only two men did not smile: Makepeace, in his commander's regard, and the other, he without truth. Even Jacobs, much farther back in the parade off the field, felt a stretch on his face, drawn and weary, if little else. His young lieutenant, Phillip Noakes, came up to greet him, and at last he found some joy.

Inside the manor neglect had begun to show. A house and grounds so large needed tending, and the workforce had been displaced. Wainscot oak was still up, as were the ornaments not yet consigned to building fires, but the hallways had taken on a clutter—supplies and paperwork— and nobody thought to dust. Some furnishings were quite grand. In the largest state room among the enfilade in back, there was a table meant for parties that came no more—in its long spread all but a promenade. Captains sat there now, lieutenants, and the three regimental colonels of the horse, foot, and gun, to make report and to talk quietly before the new man came in. None looked to the empty seat at the head, high-backed and unoccupied since Wooldridge last rode out. Jacobs had taken his customary place, just to the right. He, too, refused the urge to glance. The business of camp adjutant had been lent to his lieutenant, seated beside him, though the man had reports to share. In his distraction Jacobs cared little for the glory of reading out the news.

Makepeace entered in fresh clothes, and as one the officers rose up. None might have guessed that he had just led a rout. The miles had been shed, it seemed. Sentance and Vanderas walked in tow and stood behind, to opposite arms of the chair. One was uneasy in the other's company but held his ground. And once the commander was in his chair—no longer an empty sight—all sat.

The general took his time. "I'd feared this seat might strike a man dumb. The loss is hard to bear. Nobody need praise a giant for his weight or thank him for his stature. I hope only to lend a hand until the threat is done with. Thanks and blessings to you all for such receipt. In circumstances such as these, it's a strong tonic indeed."

The officers assented, knocking on the tabletop. "Hear, hear," many said.

"I've reviewed the standing orders. The tactics are perfect, of course. No Scot could hope to greet our downstream kin unawares or cross the Lune without getting wet. River traffic is open, now that Lancaster's ours, and the inlet south of Blackpool should be secure in short turn, and with it the Ribble. What news of the south?"

With a bow Lieutenant Noakes rose, and if the table held a game of cards the simper alone would have told aces. He said, "My general, Preston is ours."

The applause came back, doubly loud, as Makepeace beamed. He leapt upright, clapping along. Jacobs felt a smile come and go on the deadweight of his face.

The general was seated again, and Noakes went on. "The port is secured, and all routes to the Irish Sea stand open. With the fall of the Royalists inland—lately at Clitheroe—our messengers are making speed. We've already seen a packet boat."

No eye was on Vanderas, and none saw the heed, sudden and eager.

"The next comes tomorrow, sirs," Noakes went on, "with mail and the payroll. It was the first that brought us word of Preston, and of more. Once affairs down that way are in order, Old Ironsides himself will be with us, come overland, and with all his regiments of horse. They scarcely lost three hundred men to the Cavaliers."

Applause again, nearly harsh for joy. Attentions rose once more, this time with Sentance—on a turn to Noakes.

"Our champion?" Makepeace said, seated anew. "Most delightful, and no less a surprise. Let's set a mug out for Black Tom as well." Laughter all around—and for reasons of his own Vanderas joined in. "He's hemmed them at Colchester," the general said. "Behind the walls suppers are down to candles and soap. Once Fairfax takes the news up here, he might see fit to send Lord Goring a goose."

Good for yet another laugh, however that son of an earl might have felt about the siege. For his part Vanderas could only resent a trap—nothing but foes all around, brought where he was—and soon after he took news to Róis, the escape to be.

"Irish Sea, for all love," she said in reply. The two had a scullery to themselves. "You know I couldn't return, Joaquim." Night had fallen.

"Forget 'Irish.' It's the sea part you should hear. A packet boat is fast—small and feisty as a smuggler's cat. More—from afar and under the right flag, it belongs there, yes? No stops, no suspicions. Lancaster is downriver. We'd reach it in but a day and pass through without trouble. The Englishes, they put their minds south, on Preston. But once in saltwater we could get to a port, and there cross the ocean."

"With what to buy the fare?"

"Treasure. It's a packet boat—it brings the pay. Think, Sadbh—the West Indies. That Virginia Charter. New France. Acadia. Massachuser Bay. There's little on paper out there—a lot of undrawn map. Any name you bring, it will be yours for a lifetime. I can't think of a better place for two people who want to go forgot."

Róis thought. "Nothing worse than what we've known, aye."

"I'll take you. Whatever you'd have of me. I know you've no love of a husband, but if you let me, you'd have another. I'd plead it—beg."

Many things showed in her at once—shock, amusement, even a mistrust.

"Plead," he said again, faltering. "Beg." He took a knee, and with a shake of the head she looked away. "No, Sadbh.

106

With you I'd do no wrong. And without you I'd stay a bastard, though a better one for having known you at all."

"Stop, stop," she said. "It's too much, you dunce. And for God's sake, that name—it's unlucky. It's a thing for a headstone." But her eyes were filling with tears, even though she found it glib, silly, this knee on the floor, this betrothal. "A chroí, a stór—marriage? What church would have us? What God, for all love?"

"First things first. There's a boat to steal, and a lot of coins."

"So we go from murderers to thieves."

"Kidnappers as well. We'll need the crew."

She smiled to a corner of her mouth. "Hostage-takers. Well, it is a step up."

"Small but in the right way. In time we'll be all but saints."

He had watched the smirk die and mistook the cause. But her eye had moved past him. On a turn he saw Sentance in the door. His hand shot to the hilt, but she caught the wrist and held his eye with a firm refusal.

Sentance had not moved. "Conspire as you like," he said at last. "But I'll have a word alone—with her."

Vanderas said, "Listening, Sentance? Did that ear need a scratching?"

"Róis," Sentance said—no draw, no move, so at last Vanderas let go of his backsword. Róis touched his face. A nod sent him away, with glances back.

"There's no surprise you'd like to part," Sentance said.

"Shouldn't take a fancy, Niall. Or shall I call you by the Dutch name?"

"There's a chore for you—a last chore. And after, we might be rid of one another."

Despite a mistrust—only wise—Róis couldn't help but listen. The crime was laid out, in brief, up in Makepeace's new bedchambers once Sentance led her there. Months had gone in a cold crawl—a ghost's life—but in mere days it seemed that hope could outweigh a risk.

What was left of the general's old regiments had set up tents nearer to the river. There they celebrated with their newfound comrades, who did not stint with ale. Fires were going, so many that the air never took on a nip, however deep the night.

Captain Jacobs was amid that reprieve—music, laughter, drink—but had gone to a corner. A mug had been put in his grip, but there in the shadow he never had a taste. The revelry all about—songs, happy voices, a fiddle playing out a jig—was no more than oblivion. Instead he thought, and thought, and to no end, and the rough feel of crust and stone was vivid in his hand even as he held the smooth vessel and the beer went flat.

"As before?"

Makepeace was in bedclothes but up on his feet. Sentance had by the door. "No," the general said. "So close another high-placed death would raise questions.

Wooldridge had friends under the scoutmaster general, many friends, and not all of them were mine as well. It wouldn't matter how natural it seemed. No—this time, it must go at a remove. Perhaps on the road south, some country inn."

"A slow dose then. Typically it's given over time, in food or drink."

"Nothing in one ministration would do the work?"

Róis considered it. "Not singly. But a combination , if taken on the same stomach—a measure in the wine, a measure in the food. Two parts made whole in the victim himself. I know the agents, but if one met the other on the tongue, while chewed or drank down, there would be a taste, a strong taste—like pepper and honey it's told. Not bitter of itself, but plain and startling."

"But even then it would be too late?"

"The insides of a mouth will do. Nothing after would change the course, no. Bleeding, blue stone, any other physic would go in vain. Over time the body grows weak. Hair falls out, teeth. At last he can't hold anything down or in. A wet demise, and horrible, like drowning abed."

Makepeace listened to his paces on the floor. "Grisly, yes—but decisive. I'd hardly think a craftswoman had qualms, but know you this, Róis. The man is no Fairfax. Nor even a Wooldridge. His conscience is a venal thing— no more fast on him than a codpiece. And uniform aside, he's no soldier. He's a man for politics."

"Much as you then."

"Deem it as you like," he said after a pause. "I know my goodwill. In time you might, too, albeit from afar, once the change is known abroad. Where you've gone then, this be done, that's your own affair. None could say just at what hour he'll arrive. Best to stand ready. You can fix this right away? Tonight?"

"All's in store, aye. But afar you say? Truly, Makepeace?"

"Never trouble me; I'll return the favor. The rival gone, Black Tom will appoint me to the vacancy, right beneath him. Second in command of all armies. Fairfax is virtue itself—to a fault, mayhap. There will be no doubts, nor need to allay them. He's a true soldier of the realm, whoever holds the seat. Years ahead, the worst past—and any else who vie for rule—I'll see less need of compromise."

The final word made the distaste plain. Fear morálta, Róis thought, with an old stir—an urge to make the cross. She took her leave.

Some virtue was above question, yet here sat Captain Miles Jacobs, in the dark, contemplating murder. He had put the mug aside, on a crate, and the bubbles had shrunk down to a film. Fellow soldiers kept up the revels all around, though it grew late, and those not lost to a stumbling dance before the fiddles shared in tales of war.

Jacobs did as well—old mind to new. "He'll ride with you," Makepeace had said. "So doing he'll earn a measure of humanity." Yards had been the reply, but a different gauge was now at work—a tally. That was the best accounting for Vanderas. How many to that figure, Jacobs asked himself. And how many that he knew.

He looked to the celebration. As a professional man at arms he had seen every kind of band and army, from militia to king's guard. The contempt felt by Loyalists to the men they named Roundheads was no secret—the insult had, in truth, become something of a badge or honor. Look at them all, Jacobs thought, same as ever. Merchants, blacksmiths, farmers, farriers tanners, ordinary souls in pot helmet, russet coat, and buff, happy as could be. And too often, no matter who had the charge of them, they were served out as grist.

The years had been a short count since the first outbreak of war—six, just six. But more time than that was shown on Jacobs, far more, and not just for the smite. He had been fresh indeed back then, and even freer with bawdy jokes—a levy of the foot, not yet officer. His outfit had been short pike and musket, and neither had favor at the time. Approaching the bridge had put him among several dozen, likewise armed and cautious. The enemy had withdrawn across Gaddis Stream when the Parliamentarians had seen reserves come in to aid them. Behind Jacobs and his comrades all the earth was torn up from the fight, and all the air stank of it. Men still lay in mud, Roundhead and Cavalier alike, along with many horses. Embers were smoldering yet, and some way back forces were being marshaled for the push. Jacobs's vanguard had been ordered to secure the bridge. A straightforward task—it was early medieval and small, scarcely wide enough to permit a modern axle-tree. People long gone had dropped stones into a greening arch. For necessity—the waterway was far more a hazard than it seemed, a stream in name alone. The gap was just wide enough to frustrate a leap, whether from horse or man, and though it seemed an easy wade—a churn of white and dark water combing through heads of rubble—the depth was unknown. In truth a river laid there to a side in a deep fissure. The water it spoke in the usual plash but with a low thunder underneath, more felt through the soles than heard.

As Jacobs and the others came up to the bridge— the far end lost behind the steep bow—they saw a small party just past. They were on horseback and flew the blue—king's colors. In the middle was their commander-in-chief. Any man in England could have named him on sight, even without the ensign. Prince Rupert of the Rhine, with an advisor close at his ear. The Cavaliers raised no arms, made no move to flee, just past the range of a shot. No white was up for parley or surrender, but it could have meant nothing else.

The Roundhead musketeers felt a thrill at the chance— a decisive catch. Those higher up would want a chance for interrogation. So they slung the firearms and took up pikes as their group tapered onto the span. No more than three or four could walk abreast with room left to fight or in truth to sidle much at all. Jacobs and two others had the lead—old friends of his from the trained bands. As they crested, a figure came into view, crouched at the far end. And once they had sight of him, he came onto his feet—a swart man, black-haired, and abhorrent in his filth. Clothes lay in rot upon him, caked in dry blood and offal. Under matted hair, eyes glistened, and the green in them stood out from the red like corrosion. In one hand was a ceramic jug, in the other that famous backsword, already drawn. The knives in his baldric were polished to a shine—with the long blade, the only kempt things on his person.

Jacobs and his comrades hesitated but were not yet afraid, not of a lone beggar, sword or none. With a look to one another, each gave a nod, and with pikes up they stepped forward.

The jug was slung aside. Wine drained from the shards on the paving stones, and Jacobs could remember the rank acid waft of it with utter clarity. His throat caught at the stink, six years run out, and he had lost the taste for wine. The drunkard gave a call, if that were how to name the sound that tore from the throat. Not anger, not a cry for battle, but a madness. Jacobs could hear it now, above the fiddle scrape. The inhumanity had gone unheeded. Three dozen men on one—slung to their backs, the muskets they might have kept ready.

How that choice had worn on the captain—pole arms brought out in favor of gun. The mistake had driven him to hone his aim, but aim or none, it should have made the difference. Perhaps. Instead he had looked past, to the Cavaliers, wondering at their game. All had turned their faces, save for Rupert and his advisor. Even at the time this had struck him as odd, and something about it tickled at him yet. Those king's men who looked away had known what would come next, and on seeing the dread of the enemy, Jacobs could have warned his comrades off. Perhaps.

The swordsman charged the span. Jacobs was yet at the head. He watched the free hand go to the baldric, even as the mercenary spun into them. Like a wheel thrown free of a wreck—backsword and knife flashed, and the pikes were nudged out of true. On a blow Jacobs's nearest friend crashed into him, pressed him to the railing, and he saw that the mouth had been slashed open to the join. Screaming, eyes wild, the lower row of teeth a hoof print in blood. Past the eyes the fore part a hand flew free, taken at the knuckle. Jacobs had shoved his friend aside, his dying friend, to raise the pike. The horror only grew the more he saw: armaments and body parts flown loose, the assailant and his backsword in a frenzy. Fingers, hafts of pike, ears, teeth yet on the gum. He turned to the line and saw a living face hung like wash, this from a cavity of skull bone; he saw a man running without hands, a cheesecloth bulge inside a gaping belly wound; and he saw worse—all of it methodical, deliberate, and too quick to follow. Through the mayhem screams came, men unable to retreat against those amassed behind them. Desperate, struck thoughtless, Jacobs lunged with his pike and there lost half the world. A flash, a moment lost, saw him looking up from the stones in wan light, with nothing felt but the sting of blood in the one eye he had left. His head had struck the railing, he was later told, and this was the least of his damage. In his chest a throwing knife was sunk to the hilt. Seeing it he batted weakly, unable to keep a grip. Sound was muffled, vision tinted yellow, and blood ran freely from the knot of men. A friend crept into view minus a leg and an arm, pulling with the hand he had to him. Jacobs tried to rise, fell as his hand slipped on wet stones, to a side, eye to the butchery. Drafts of gunsmoke were in his mouth and nose and he saw the clouds drifting on the air. Fire from the Roundheads' side of the water—some had taken aim at the lone fighter. In the tangle, and with a fluid target, they had only managed to shoot their own. From rail to rail the men were a deadfall, branches of limb and pike. In the space between them and Jacobs, the fallen. Some fought to worm away, some for a breath. In the disarray soldiers reeled back, tripping over one another, overcome with fright, and the man whose name Jacobs had yet to learn stepped among them. With care now, hacking off what he could—selecting prizes. The men dropped weapons and raised hands, only to present a target. Surgeon's work—he blinded them, slashed through jaws, gelded them, all with a nimble move and a mad precision.

Mad—madness itself. He never told another soul as much, not even his wife down in London, but Jacobs had turned away then, from the men he knew back to the party of Cavaliers. Too much to bear, all seen—but the horror read there, too, on the faces of the enemy. Some wept, and none could watch for long, save the man in charge, the figure at his side, where assay was steady and cold.

The yellowness went pale as Jacobs came to death. Except that he woke in time, come back from an empty silence, as he did now from memory.

Fury built, to a tremble like fever. He saw that he had passed something like an hour unawares. The soldiers were done with the fete and save for a few merry stragglers had gone off to tents and bedrolls. The mug was yet there, untouched until the sweep of his hand struck it from the crate. A detachment was on him. He watched himself take his feet. On the walk through camp, he knew the mistake even as he made it. Ahead, slumped in the aisle between tents, he saw a Roundhead musketeer on guard duty. Hardly breaking stride, he snatched the man's sidearm out from the hilt. He sped to a trot, then a run, then a reckless sprint, sword in hand, never with a sense of being in himself.

At his strumpet's side—that was where to find the renegade. The men posted outside the house knew the camp adjutant, of course. Even as he flung wide the doors—as for assault—they did not bar the way. Nor did they move from their post as the look of alarm built— not until they heard the name shouted there in the foyer.

"Vanderas!"

All his breath wrung on it—a rousing cry. The guards came in, half-pike ready. But they glanced to each other in reluctance even as they watched Jacobs run. To the foot of the main stairway he went, and between doors in the hall, with no more sure course than a ransacker. Officers quartered there had begun to poke heads out and step into the open, dressed only in their shirts.

"Vanderas! Come out I say!"

The anguish brought notice to more than those captains. Sentance stood by an unlit doorway—to the master suite upstairs—with an ear to the racket on the ground floor. "Be ready," he said to the general, once the door stood open. Makepeace was sitting up in bed and he, too, had heard.

A man long under Wooldridge was adjutant to the house itself. Once he came into the hall, the guards flanked him, and the company stood as one before Jacobs, weapons ready, to block his way. "Sir, what is the meaning of this?"

Jacobs shouted past. "Come out! Coward! Come out!"

Here Makepeace made the landing, Sentance behind. He had put on his breeches and a face. "Jacobs, have you lost your wits? Are you drunk? Disarm yourself and cease this noise or I'll have you in irons."

The sword came down but not the temper. "A spy, sir. There's a spy among us—an agent for the Royalists—and without fault,"—spoken to the officers—"it, it was the general who let him here."

All eyes went to Makepeace.

"A spy?" he said. "Vanderas? There are subtler agents, wouldn't you say?

"We speak of a butcher," Jacobs went on, "he at Gaddis and the cruelty on the bridge, now in this very house. Our general could not have known, but I'll have no more. Our friends at arms — it's a blemish on their memory. I'll have done with it for all our sakes."

"Why do you say spy?" the general asked.

"I won't speak more to that, not here. I can't. For all the certainty there's no proof. Do as you should, sir, but the challenge will stand, and I'll have an answer—call him out, even in forfeit of warrant, freedom, life."

"Miles, please—put the weapon down. Let's discuss it. I'd sooner send away a man for hire than an officer like you."

The house captain spoke up. "General, is this so? The butcher of Gaddis, here?" Rumors had spread, but the men on that post had only thought it game.

"So and true, or so I've heard."

This was Vanderas, standing behind. He was unarmed and had put on breeches to come up from the cellars—breeches and nothing else. Hay from a rude bedding was stuck about his hair and even on his sweat. The eyes fell on him—surprise, then worse—and he said, "What was it you had to say, Jacobs?"

The house guard, to a man, had stepped away from the captain. That room made, none would have stopped him then and there. But the general said, "Do as I ask. Go at him like this, strike him undefended, and you're no better. Grief is clouding your judgment. Clifford was like a father to you. Damn you, Miles—drop your sword!"

The clatter came late, but Jacobs had listened. Though it was with far less hesitation that he stepped closer to Vanderas, pulling a glove. Gage thrown, he said, "Satisfaction. If anything in you resembles bravery, we'll meet on the commons. First light, before this army."

Vanderas looked to the glove at his feet, to Jacobs, the faces set against him, and again to Jacobs. But it was to Sentance, just behind it all, that he spoke.

"First light."

With no further remark he retreated from these, his most recent allies, left to their anger. None would look to Makepeace, least as Jacobs took his own leave. "You'll have my letter, sir," he said as he made for the door, no mind to he in command or to the figment that did his work.

Vanderas had neither left the house nor went back to the must underneath, not at first. His pastimes seldom ran to taking in a view, or to thoughtfulness, but he found himself on the roof, alone with both. A parapet walk skirted the brick, and he found a place to look past the earthworks and the crude ramparts. The scheme of tents outside the redoubt was a patchwork of lamplight. Commons, Jacobs had said, which could only mean the field just beyond. A view of what lay ahead, a choice to weigh—Vanderas could only see that his talents lay elsewhere.

Back to the cellars, then, the vault full of casks and a stink of grape. It brought no thirst, no fond memory of wine. Checking the contents had not once occurred to him, although, dry or not, thought of drink had never strayed far in five years without it. He walked past the sour stores to a torch bracket, the only patch of eyesight. Past this Róis had set up shop. All her lockboxes had been brought down, the strange machinery taken out. Shadow was so deep in that corner that nothing was shown save a lone ring of candle flame, bluish and dim. "Stay back," he heard her shout, though her voice was muted. Her breath had a rasp as if drawn through a reed. Though unseen, her hands were yet busy, and he

119

heard metal on ceramic—a stir. "Palsy in ants," she said, though he could not make it all out. "For agony, slow to fast, there's liquor of a mushroom. Webcap, death cap, destroying angel. In rye there's madness, and laughter can be scraped off from the backs of frogs. God's doing, mind you, but churchgoers take it for witchcraft, and small wonder."

The last of this he caught, and he said, "No hag was ever so grateful to the eye."

Soon she was closer to the torchlight, visard yet on, pouring a stream from a jug down hands and forearms, one at a time. He had never seen the mask and as she stood out from the dark he took a shock. Beneath that dear frame of hair there was no face, no feature, aside from two pitted eyes. A journey through hells might fetch him such a glimpse—some denizen come to the river bank to watch a ferry pass her by. "Aqua vitae," Róis said, without notice, "pure from the still. There's a residue and this cleanses it off. Though it seems a waste of good whiskey." Down came the mask, to a tuck at an elbow, where it haunted him yet. Keenly he felt what he could not name. To take him by the arm for assurance—misreading the unease, perhaps—she let the jug fall and spill. "They'll let me go. That boat of yours, we can ride it out without fear of chase. We needn't even be thieving the damned thing."

"That's glad, amor meu, that's glad." Two on the boat, rid of these depths. The ferry would not go on alone—he would see it. They embraced. The tremble in her was delicate but plain—relief, hopes—and neither would be dashed, not by his like.

"Our plan's still fair," she said into his shoulder, and her breath spread warm. "He asks we go far. But once the two of us cross the sea we needn't take such pains. New lives, a stor, without care of leaving a back turned. One last ugliness and it's done. Though I'll be at it yet tonight."

"Work in store?"

"Hours, hours. Keep the straw warm. Aye, that'll sleep me like a saint."

As had the field cot for Miles Jacobs, to his surprise. Once come back to his tent, he had drafted a letter of resignation, and another more painful. Slipping off boots, he had lain with no drowsiness in a rambling thought. Yet now, before the first break, he came to—by himself, no cockcrow or tolling bell to prompt him—feeling only better. On went his best clothes, a black doublet that was almost proud. Upon the cot a basket sword waited as he drew ribbon through eyelet, and he had slung no firearm. Then he went to a knee, and to prayer, asking nothing, giving thanks.

In came Makepeace. He, too, was in fine dress. "Forgive the intrusion."

"My notice is on the table."

The general did not take up the letter, nor turn. He stared, measuring a word. "I haven't done right by you, Miles. I wish to apologize."

"Sir, I could never doubt that all you've done, every part, you saw as right."

Makepeace's eye had gone to the sword. "He couldn't match your skill. Would that duels were fought by pistol."

"It was fear that made a marksman—fear and the horror of that day. With a rifle I've stood myself off, as I have ever since." Jacobs put the sheath locket to his belt.

"Your family will take an annuity — your baby girl, your wife." Mention of family brought a wince. Out in the muck and the heartbreak, Jacobs never spoke of what he held dear. But here the news was good, even if it made him think of what he had tried to put down in the second letter, to failure. He cinched up cloak to shoulders as Makepeace went on. "And they'll have my protection, I swear it. You're one of the finest soldiers I've known, Miles. One of two."

Jacobs gave a nod. With no further pause or word he left the tent. Skies had only begun to take color and bright planets were still out, but there was ample light to see that he was far from alone. Jacobs gave a start and looked back to all those many faces, proud and solemn, hundreds of them in the surround. His friends at arms, in finery with hats off. By tradition they had brought their weapons along—halfpike, blade, pistol, and musket. The salute shimmered on a tear in his eye, but the breeze recruited him, brisk cold flown down from the north. He took the lane made for him and him alone. Behind he heard the shuffle of boots on dew and grass—otherwise a ritual silence, not a word spoken.

Beside the tent, and Makepeace's own horse, Sentance was on a bay, red with dark muzzle. The general mounted up and the two rode at a walk behind the flood tide of soldiers. The chosen ground was not far ahead, where two shallow hillocks met. Vanderas was there, backsword ready, small in the fold.

He watched them come: Jacobs in the lead, clad in a priestly black, and all regiments behind. The latter split to fan out on the slopes, and the captain came to a halt thirty paces off—that lone eye never straying from the opponent—and with far more calm to show, it seemed, than a degenerate drunkard who had lost count of rape and death.

Jacobs held ground as his comrades filled the grass. Soon it was like a theater round, tightly packed with spectators, all mum. Vanderas looked away from that mob to Jacobs again. Makepeace and Sentance had ridden up to a halt immediately behind. No heat in that ravaged face, not like the night before, only a patience.

"You brought no second, Jacobs?"

A lame try, but the captain lent a smile. "And you?"

"No friends near," Vanderas said.

"Do you truly recall nothing of the bridge? Nothing of what you did?"

"Oh I'll answer, Captain. I'll answer, memory or none."

"In part. You'll answer in part."

"Well told." Pat as it seemed Jacobs took little notice of the remark, what it hinted at, and he drew his sword. But Vanderas had weighed the task, and he gathered the nerve to see it done. "Déu meu," he said. "This is going to hurt."

"Cross swords," Makepeace called out.

Jacobs raised his, stepping up, as Vanderas did the backsword. One blade touched the other, tip on tip, and where they met the backsword gave a rattle. Vanderas did not see the Roundheads smile, intent as he was, but he felt the contempt for his shaking grip. No matter—they were mistaken. Jacobs gave no sign of conceit, only met the gaze. They held the pose, no relent to the nervous quaver.

The general drew a breath to shout. "Begin!" And even before finish on the word Jacobs found skies reeling, the weapon flown from his grip, the ground come up to snatch him. On the sword hand there was a nick at the thumb, and he only felt it once he caught a breath and heard the crowd react.

He looked up, looked for the sword, looked to Vanderas, who only stood in place. The nerves had grown no calmer, it seemed, though victory was sure. Once the two men were looking at each other, a jab planted the backsword in the earth.

Vanderas had disarmed himself. The crowd muttered, and he fell to knees, hands to his back, looking to the captain. It was the posture of a bound victim, no bonds to be seen. Jacobs took his feet. The basket sword lay in the grass between them.

"Have an eye, Jacobs," Vanderas said.

"What—"

"Thumb or stab as you choose. But if by a smaller blade you'd have my thanks."

Jacobs grew closer, and the crowd listened in. "Your thanks?"

"For the debt. I won't raise a hand. I won't resent it. This bridge you spoke of, you walked off it, though deprived. Deprive me the same way. Yes? I think it's something from the Bible. Vengeance, holy bloodwit, name it what you like."

Jacobs understood—and was far from pleased. "No. It's too little. Take up your weapon. Your offenses, they're more than a piece could pay."

"Yet where eyes go I've only got the two. One tab at a time, Jacobs. The dead, they can wait. It's what they're best at."

"Kill him, Miles," a Roundhead cried. Others joined in, to a roar.

The captain shot up a hand. The audience fell still. He had begun to pace though had drawn no closer. "This is no haggle," he said. "We don't go to grass to make bargains. And your cruelties outcount that, that day."

"Also true. Me, I've been all over. An eye's what I owe you. Lay the scar deep. Perhaps I can boast a white lock like yours."

"And what of Wooldridge, you bastard? What would our trouble earn him?"

Every man listened, more intent than before. And even Makepeace, yet atop the horse behind Jacobs, feigned surprise.

Vanderas hid nothing, for his part. The look of puzzlement, innocence, was only pure. He shook his head. "The general?"

The tone put Jacobs in a rush. He took up the basket sword as he ran and only stopped short of slashing down. Vanderas winced but held the pose, hands behind the back. "Raise your sword, damn you," Jacobs said. "I cannot strike you so."

"Well that's a comfort."

"Captain Jacobs," Makepeace cried, loud enough for all to hear. "Fell the blackguard and none here could think the less."

And the Roundheads made their agreement plain—a hearty cheer.

But Jacobs took no swing. His comrades fell silent once again as he took a step back. Vanderas opened his eyes. Some private light had come. Jacobs did not turn to Makepeace. "Sir, that's not what you said last night."

Vanderas gave a shout, quite abrupt, and all eyes shot back. "The stink. The goddam stink of it all. Like a trollop's sores but less honest. Jacobs, all you English lot, never hear him. Listen past—there's a whisper at his ear." He stood with no move for the weapon in the turf. "Your cause is nothing to him. He cares nothing for it, or for you—he is the cause. Remember that other morning, General? When your hangman's party came back with me in uniform? Know your enemy, you said. None of the honey stuck but that." Resolve, a sneer, a look to Jacobs. "Yes. As you say, Jacobs—there was venom in the cup. Wooldridge died by that sting, as bid. My sting, my poison. But his order"—a chin to Makepeace.

A pistol, drawn in a snap from the jet cloak, was leveled on Vanderas. But no shot came. Beneath the muffler Sentance held a glance, sidelong, and gave a cock of the head. Too soon whatever had been heard was lost to the fury of the crowd. But among that outrage glances went to the general, and the doubt could only grow.

Makepeace found a face. Half blinkered he might have been, but Jacobs was nearest, and he saw the whole in that guilt, quickly hid. And what he had only just heard from the foe's mouth—in the lie told, a selfless lie—had shown him more.

No chance to ask, for here she was—she whom Vanderras had sought to protect, pushing through the ranks. She charged onto the dueling ground. Facing out before Vanderas, she stood tall but unsteady. In each grip was a knitting hook.

Her face wrung to tears, Róis cried, "Any Englishman as comes too close dies like a wretch."

Fast asleep, she had seemed, when Vanderas had risen and left the straw. He had found no repose there, only wakeful troubles, and when she came from her own long work he had shut his eyes. But he was not the only one who could feign sleep, nor whom a rueful thought could plague. What she had cooked up that night was vile, Róis knew—far worse than her other poisons. Not even a vengeful heaven would inflict such hell. She had left the vial where instructed, for retrieval, and it would not be stoppered up for long. What would happen then—to the victim—would go unseen, but she saw it play out before her eyes. In the dram she had made all that long agony had no color or scent, but was vivid to her, no less so than the present moment.

When her boyish lover took his arm away and rose, she was lost yet in the scene. As it spun she paid his departure little notice. Gone out to find the privy, sure, until a half hour had gone by, alone with gruesome fate, and she began to sense the worse.

The sight quieted the Roundheads—the dire threat of knitting hooks—but only to a puzzlement. A laugh would have built had she not said more. "There's death enough smeared on these humble tools to slay the hundreds of you."

"Róis, no!" On a leap Vanderas snatched up his backsword. He stepped between her and Makepeace, who was staring on aghast. The general took no special mind—Vanderas's eye darted from man to man in the surround, each no less a threat.

"You confess it!" Jacobs cried. "Assassin!"

Every last weapon brought out on ceremony came up fast. From that thicket eyes in multitude gave a gleam. In a choked voice, Vanderas said, "None will touch her."

But Róis came out from the defense, batting his arm aside. "Poison—of that Joaquim is innocent," she shouted to them all. "He had no part. Else was only truth. Slain on command, your general was, by Makepeace and that trespasser at his side—him you name Sentance."

Gunshot on that mention would have been no surprise, to the general least of all. But Makepeace turned to where his aide had been not a moment before. Man and horse were gone. Glancing about, and in a growing fluster, he drew his own sidearm.

"What were you told," Róis went on, "you of this army? That I was his relish, a bedroll comfort? No whore could be so blind to what befell as you. Where Wooldridge lost, who stood to gain? Even now they plot against that Cromwell—"

The clap struck out the word. A cry came back through the gout of smoke. But as it cleared Makepeace saw that he had struck not Róis but her man. Vanderas had stepped before her. He clutched himself at left shoulder and took a knee. Beneath the grumbles of the men she tore at his shirtsleeve. The hooks had been thrown aside.

Jacobs looked on the two. He had made no move since Róis ran onto the field. But at last he turned to Makepeace to weigh the accusations and saw that Sentance had gone. And he would have met the general's eye, asked whatever needed to be asked, if he had not seen an arrival, just past.

From the scrub a scout rode in, at a limping gait. The horse was bloodied, as was the man. But even for distance his eyes stood out: gaping white on a sooted face.

"All Scotland," the scout cried. "All Scotland!"

The Roundheads turned to the voice, as did Makepeace. Jacobs was running for the scout before he toppled from his seat. Too late: the man struck the grass, and with a graceless drop his animal knelt and lay on a side, heaving for breath.

Still the rider managed to warn them once again—"All Scotland"—and as Jacobs drew close, though quietly and on a retch, he said, "All Scotland is come."

"It passed," Róis was saying, speaking of the ball, "but there's too much blood. Powder. We'll need gunpowder and a flint."

Vanderas said nothing. To keep himself upright he had set a hand to the earth, and now he was intent on the spread of his fingers—what felt in the ground. "To your posts," Makepeace was shouting. "Defend the camp!" Near footfall, hundreds of men, masked the pitch of hooves—far but drawing near, and countless many.

"More than I can count or guess," Vanderas said. "Saved by the cavalry. There's a pretty picture." Despite herself Róis gave a laugh. "Let's not hold generosity against them."

"What should we do then?"

"Run for our lives."

Only Jacobs kept close. From the fallen scout he had claimed pistol and kit, and now he stood before the conspirators. Yet he took no aim, spoke no threat. "It's true," he said. "What you said is true." He gave the kit a toss: flask and tinderbox.

Vanderas and the captain held a stare as Róis took them up. Without further word Jacobs ran for his tent, the better firearm that lay within.

She packed it to the wound the powder stung, much like salt, and the pain of cautery was no less searing than the flame that cooked him shut. The yell tore, and Róis held him tight. When the rolling echo faded a signal horn could be heard—a desperate note, though faint—and behind this a low thunder.

"Poor arm," Vanderas said. "It's not been happy late."

Once he had his feet they took a hill for a look west. From between rises another Roundhead scout rode, full gallop. No wounds could show at the distance, but he and his horse had fared no better. Bolts were stuck at flank and shoulder, and the scout gathered a breath to blow the horn again.

Behind him, coming into sight, was a host of Lowland Scots on horseback, an endless column. Those at the fore had crossbow and musket and were on the scout's heels. Slow gains, but the range closed and as Vanderas watched rider and horse were cut down. The tumble was instantly swept over, and the stream of riders grew no slower for the bump.

Sky to sky, Vanderas searched about. Farther off—north and south—rising dust made sign. Thin, nothing like the cloud put up in drier parts, but it did tell of worse to come: ranks no fewer, vast in truth. Those west were only the lead—hirelings—and he looked eastward to the river bend. As yet no packet boat, no means across.

"Between here and the hills there's hardly any cover," he said, "and no way to make friends before they stamp us over. Can you swim?"

"Some. Enough." And they ran for the Lune.

*   *   *

Within stakewall and earthwork Roundheads made ready the artillery. Small arms were primed and set to racks aside pails of match. The air was grim, desperate, all those faces ashen. Jacobs had sped in, rifle and saddle slung to each shoulder, and between two comrades he found a temporary position behind an embankment, near the front. A glance to the house was all he lent to other matters. Orders would dispatch soon. Treason could wait. He watched the riders, to a frown. "They're not making for the bridge," he said.

"What could it mean, sir?" a soldier asked him.

"Nothing good for us. Noakes! Here, down here. Make ready our horse."

The tent camp had been left empty—any woodcutters and shopkeeps had made a hearty run for it on their rude awakening. At the outermost circle Jacobs saw the torches thrown, the bladders of oil strung to lines, and the canvas began to burn under Scottish jeers.

Makepeace had run inside to the charts. Around him at the table were the three regimental colonels, and they looked no less desperate than the captains outside. Reports about the bridge, the lack of Scottish interest there, had already come in. "Losses south must have driven them to us," the general said. "All those infantry at Preston. Farther upriver they can't launch for the shallows, so there won't be enemy craft. The attack is bold. They'll lose many."

"As will we," a colonel said. "It's not the crossing they want. This isn't stratagem—it's a serving. Our good position is become our trap."

Makepeace gave no sign of fear. "The artillery can make mince, but yes, in time they'll get through. None could have seen it—there's not much cavalry up there. If it's English blood they want, they'll have it."

"A word."

This was Sentance, come up beside. He had been missing on errands of his own, and in his annoyance Makepeace left caution aside. "Not now, damn you," he said, eyes to the field map. "Redouble the halfpike along—"

Thrown—Sentance had seized onto his shirt. He was held in place against a wall, held fast. "The doubt's growing," said the whisper. "They'll arrest you."

"There's more at hand. You counsel hasn't blinded me such that—"

"Clear the room," Sentance said. "You'll find the smell of your innards less bracing than courage of number. Out with them, now."

With no hem, and none of the fear shown, Makepeace spoke past. "My advisor has forgotten himself, gentlemen. He will apologize."

Sentance let go of the collars and made a turn. None had ever seen the face he made then—every semblance of shame. "I ask your pardon. The lies of that Irishwoman, they stung deep."

"Hurry now," Makepeace said to the room. "Go out and direct the cannon. Put marksmen on the roofline. Further orders will come out by dispatch, and soon."

Without a bow the colonels took their leave. No sentiment remained in the face that came close. "Send all horse to the south."

"Leave the foot exposed? They'll be killed to a man."

"To outpace the scouts, the horsemen already with us will have ridden nonstop through Westmoreland, for the firmer ground. They have the shabby look of militia—untrained—and they'll be ragged for a sleepless night. A hard charge will break through. The sign south shows a much larger force. Read the dust. On that pretense your regiments will push through—to head off the greater drove."

"Without support from the horse the men on foot couldn't—"

"You. You alone. Defense of the bridge will be the ruse. All English cavalry gone out, the Scots will strike at a single point in the redoubt to overwhelm us. One side or the other will be clear for riding out—likely the southern side. Leave the rest to the Scots, and any news of Wooldridge. Notoriety could hardly spread."

Makepeace pulled a chair from the table, and with a heartless drop he sat. "Monstrous. Purely monstrous. The Northern Association? The only defenses on the borderland?" The general stared into the cool regard. "You mean to flee as well. So. Even you can worry for a hide."

"This association is done with. Your horse will be outfitted for travel south—many days' provision. But I won't ride aside you today, nor again. Send the order."

The last words came with force, and Makepeace shrank. Here any notion of command left him, any design, and he turned away to take up the bell for messengers.

*  *  *


The Engager's infantry had been lost at Preston, it was true, but the Scots who came that day saw it more simply than that. They were angry. Since the turn on Flodden Field better than a hundred years before, where Tudor billmen had shown up the northern pike, English tactics had been a sticking point. More than that, there was the matter of a Stewart dynasty and its rightful place, and an enmity of seven hundred years. Green, fierce, and hundreds—men in trews, more without, armed by any means they could scrape up and set atop any beast from jade nag to fresh pony, here rode into view. More a mudflow, that howl and gallop, as seen from the parapets of the house and the embankments—a rainy scour broken off a summit. With an avalanche churn hooves threw clots above the head of horse and man alike. The riders swept through what remained of the tents. Cannon and heavy mortar stood ready, and all the men arrayed about the guns prayed for true aim. Fire commenced, general fire—the ringing boom of longbore and the deep thump of mortar underneath. Shockingly loud—enough so to drown out the stampede. A reek stood curling about the hill—the stench of sulfur and a roiling smoke.

Jacobs watched from his position: cannonball skidding among the fore, shearing through neck and leg. Bombs on the shorter arc burst with a stupefying applause—soot and dirt and showering coals, man and horse flung cruelly left and right, man and horse set ablaze. No scream came through, no Scottish voice, and the tumult was steady. Riders came about and ran back out of range, and all the ruin stood behind them—a cratered field paved with trampled canvas and heaped up with casualties.

Loud even from a distance, that awful bombardment. Vanderas looked back from the riverbank. The sight was all too familiar, but ever new. "No sign of the packet," he said, peering downriver. "Doubtful they'd land in this weather anyway, not without the Parliamentary ensign gone up to daub their brows." He had spied a thick log washed up in the gravel, and he took up an end.

"What are you doing?" Róis said.

"It floats." He cast the end into the water. "Grab a hold."

"You'd have us paddle out on a bit of rubbish?"

"I'd have you. My arm's sprung, whatever good it would do me. I can't swim, not a lick. Let the current take you. You'll see the boat. What sailor wouldn't stop for such a nymph?"

"If you think this nymph as you name her would leave you to your peril, you're in a sadder state than Ulysses at the mast."

"Who? What? Go, Róis. I won't see you risk your neck."

"My neck was a hangman's itch long afore we met."

"Enough. Catch a hold." The log had begun to drift, inching to the channel. She had not moved and in truth had crossed her arms. "Hear that?" he asked. The tone grew short. "The pitter-pat of their firearms? The Scots are close. Smell the wool. Onto the log, bogtrotter."

"Ah, pinching it from the British now, so you are. Surely there's insult wherever it was that saw the likes of you pupped out. You're no husband of mine—not yet, Joaquim Vanderas—and if you mean to be I'll have you know I'd make a willful kind of wife, one who as the mood strikes her might forgo to ride a fucking log."

"Would I'd found a switch instead."

"And then I'd learn you the meaning of switch, you black diego bastard."

It built from there and sped to a vehemence, with English left behind—Romance and Gaelic tongues, incomprehensible, though rich in curses—even as three Scottish cavalrymen on horseback swept the bank behind them to the south.

Vanderas saw them first. He took Róis by the shoulders as the derogation went on and forced a duck. One horseman had a musket, and he fired, riding through the cloud. The shot sang past, and the two other Scots drew sabers on the charge.

No lefthand throw to work with, but distance gave Vanderas time to shy twice with the right and draw the backsword. The lead Scots took knives in the throat, and the horses ran on, saddles clear. The third came on with a snap and a fierce eye, raising the spent musket for a club.

Soon it was in Róis' hands, with amazement at what she had seen dealt out. The third riderless horse joined the other two, past reach. "Let's quarrel later, acushla." From the dragoon she took up the shot bag. A dirk was fastened to the strap.

"Strange tactic," Vanderas was saying, with a searching eye. "Clearing the bank ahead of the charge." Nothing showed across the way, nor up or down the watercourse. Whatever the aims had been, it meant one thing. "More will come."

"To the landing," she said. "Perhaps there's a rowboat. There's a shed for one up on the staithe, so I saw."

He did not know the word, but the rest was a beam. "Be damned to the packet then." Once she had bag and musket slung, Vanderas took her hand. The free grip kept the dirk, and they ran together. Such was their marriage, their short elopement.

The bombardment went on: big guns alone, and deafening, to keep a curtain down. Men with small arms held their fire and kept low. Not just for the order—there was something new to fear.

Of the thousand horse come out of the west, many lay mauled and dead on the cratered field. The cavalry had spread out, seeming reluctant to add onto the butcher's bill, but in truth they had only bided time. Drawing near were the late arrivals: from the north rode two thousand more, and these were Highland ranks, one and all. Bearded men and clan kilt, with animals bred for speed and fearlessness, and no strangers to open war. It was true there had never been much formal Scottish cavalry, and this was all of them, comprised of men who had sported on one another for centuries just to keep in prime against the English. The redoubled forces began to circle the entire grounds at a hearty clip. Shell and fuze were out of range, but the fire kept on. Dust looming to the south told of the next arrival, wherever those Stuart men had been levied or bought. Soon they would join their Lowland kin, and all the pony rabble had to do was wait.

Behind the Roundhead defenses captains of the horse awaited orders from the colonel. They and their men were mounted and ready to enter the fray, and all looked taut for the privilege. Jacobs had saddled up and joined his own cohort. The adjutant had charge of the base-bound scouts, who were most often sent on local patrol. But light horse could serve well enough as skirmishers— three hundred, no more.

Messengers brought the orders to the colonels, and seals were broken all at once. Three captains met what they heard with shock, Jacobs with a flush of anger. He knew what poor decisions bought, and who would pay. Held up high enough for his skirmishers to see, the page was torn to quarters and thrown aside. As camp adjutant he did not answer to regimental colonels, and the call was his, mutiny though it be. "We'll defend the musket and artillery," he shouted to them and to Noakes through the peal of guns. "Keep inside the perimeter. All make ready for close combat."

Jacobs looked on as the other captains of the horse led companies out to the south. The hoofbeats were a deep hum in the gaps of cannon fire.

"A king has never looked better," he said to himself.

The troop rode out to the Lowland enemy, and in they drove. Those at the fringes were instantly down—tangles of pike and hoof. There were not many trained war riders among those Scots, but they had numbers, even where the English and their animals stood at a thousand each. Bombardment fell off to make way, and in the confusion detachments of Scots came through. Two hundred, perhaps, charging the stakewalls with oil slings and torch. Roundheads opened with musket fire but most were unscathed, and soon anything wooden and in range of a toss was set alight.

"To the breach!" Jacobs cried. With saber and carbine three hundred skirmishers drove the riders into the burning palisades. Jacobs charged in with them, slashing in a fury. Horses ran out white-eyed and riderless, many with wounds of their own—ribcages exposed, flanks laid raw. To repel the enemy the fusiliers had resumed fire, and Jacobs felt his very wits go deaf between his ears.

The last Lowland Scots yet on horse broke off the attack and rode back out into the field. Some of Jacobs' men gave pursuit, but he shouted, "Fall in! Hold the ground! Leave them to the guns!" Roundhead musketeers were cutting them down already, and horses that made it farther out were butchered in the mortar fire. A Scottish horn sounded to recall the riders, and to chase the regiments making south.

Makepeace had put on scout's gray dress and a deep-brimmed hat to obscure his face. The horse Sentance had left at the railed terrace could haul quite a load, and at a run—saddlebags and panniers stuffed fat—but the days' provisions were not yet there and he had not been given leave. Makepeace came up to the rail. Black smoke was churning from the redoubt, and fires leapt among the outermost stakes. To protect the winding approach soldiers of the foot were packed in tight among the mounds and ditches. And the throat of artillery spoke loudest of all, to where the Scots kept a circling herd. None of that pandemonium had touched the manor house yet—the rail had not lost so much as a chip. But the roar and stink and ashen taste of what Makepeace had wrought was right before him, and otherworldly in his sight. No infernal realms could be more strange than war.

Makepeace bided, looking on the ruination of his plans. He had been told to stay, and though Sentance was nowhere near—whatever he might have got to in that disaster—Makepeace knew better than to disobey.


Vanderas and Róis kept to the bank, the cover it provided, but nearer the grounds of the house it grew shallow, just where the Lowlanders were thickest. They kept hunkered down, hearing hoofbeats and voices when cannon allowed.

But the horn was blown, and most of the Scots nearby regrouped to chase the English riders.

Lucky, perhaps—save that the horn also drew six who had ridden from the south along the watercourse. A man and a woman skulking there would not be not hard to spot. But they were haggard, those six, and had not come with the Lowlanders. In hoarse voices they shouted after their fellows to come back. Some sort of news carried up, a warning—it bought Vanderas time.

"Be a dear and fresh up that musket," he said.

Róis already had the ramrod out. To free the hand she had jabbed the dirk into the river silt. "Mean to shoot them?"

"For you to. Gunplay makes a clod of me. Had I brought a long bow ..."

"To the field of honor? What next, a handgun?"

The charge was past range, and the six newcomers looked despondent. Vanderas wondered at their trouble but did not glance away.

"Why don't they follow?" Róis said.

No time: one man spotted them and alerted his fellows. All drew sabers.

"Well there's a treat," Vanderas said, standing up. "They're out of shot."

Róis had never fired a musket before, but the work was no mystery, and the distance no special challenge. She squeezed the trigger, the powder barked, and the lead Scot fell off his horse. The rest came hard.

"Crouch down!" Vanderas said. Róis was reloading with a panic. He sprang up onto the bank, keeping low himself. A fetlock was the target, and the horse screamed

142

and threw its rider. Two horses immediately behind were tripped up, and the riders leapt free. The last two veered off and rode to a distance to come about.

Vanderas was already on the three nearest, and the work was quick. To face the last two he stood up, arms wide. They had dismounted, seeing a charge was futile. "Save that shot," he said to Róis, and to them, much louder, "We're no enemy! We're not with the goddam Englishers. I wouldn't have struck if you hadn't."

"Gies a kiss then," said a Scot. He and his friend were crofters and looked it, dressed in all but barley sacks, but fighters or not they had no use for cowardice. Parliamentarian horns had begun to sound within the defenses, just past sight.

"Let us flee," Vanderas said, to no use. They drew closer. "I don't suppose it would do to tell you—" Already they were charging in. He whirled with his backsword and a look of displeasure, then finished the thought. "—you don't stand a chance."

With a glum face he wiped the blade clean. The horns had not let up, and he gave a glance to the signal. Salvos of artillery had fallen off, and now they returned.

"Poor bastards," Róis said. "They were doing the Lord's work today. Don't let the horses suffer." Two had run clear, but the others were whinnying in anguish where they lay broken-legged.

The distaste was no less, once done. "There were times I wouldn't have pitied a man, nor even a horse."

From the direction of the Lowland Scots came a grisly roar, hundreds of voices rising up, and both their heads snapped to it. Even for the distance it was loud, tolling through the landscape. Unnerving—more so for the unknown cause.

"Let's try those two," she said, pointing to the near animals. One stared on as they came, and though the other was more skittish, there was no try to flee. "They seem tame enough."

As Vanderas and Róis got close enough to mount the horses lay down.

"Not tame," he said. "Tired out. Ridden hard."

He looked to her as she trailed off—"They had news for their friends"—and followed her eye downriver. The packet had rowers but had raised a sail to borrow speed. From afar the bright cloth was small but no less angelic a standard to fugitives from justice.

Vanderas laughed. "I take back everything I ever said about the courage of Protestants. Those six, they must have seen the boat. Let's get to the landing. The Scots have thinned out on this front. Whatever they've got to over yon."

So had the Roundheads, it seemed. Ahead, inside the perimeter, were the storehouses and the small pier and boathouse. Behind a deep trench work a barricade crossed the bank, extending into the river. The parapet on the far side did not seem to be manned.

"I don't know, Joaquim," she said as they moved. "It struck me more as a bad sort of news, so it did, and judging from the horses, come up a ways." She realized she had left the dirk behind, standing in the bank. No time for going back. There was no shortage of knives thereabout.

"All news is bad news today," he said. "Save for love of a boat to steal."

Riverside posts had been left vacant, it was true, and only moments before. What had drawn most of the soldiers off was the company horns, blown all at once, at the coming of the Highland riders from the north.

This was no common army, so long the practice up there, but a professional troop. Montrose had assembled them for the last uprising, and they served on without him. Never many in number, not by the reckoning of standing troops, but here they had come all at once, two thousand, to check losses of infantry at Preston. The royal teuchters, the Lowland recruit called them, and they saw them in with a howl and a clap of weapons on targes. The Highland riders gave back such throat that it cut even through the fusillade, and Roundhead blood ran cold. Some fiend had thought to bring along a stand of pipes. The skirl rang and a clannish song was taken up, Goidelic more shouted than sung—warping on the mile but all too close.

Even this was not the full of their taunt. The English saw the colors rise, and even from the redoubt they read the message. What flew was the ensign of personal rule, a Stuart device, the St. Andrew and the St. George commingled as one. Commonly this was only shown at sea; here it was an affront. More, it was the white saltire that stood before the red cross—the Union flag, and Scottish first.

Yet a joke: Jacobs looked past the ravaged field with something near to laughter. The hills were dark, and the darkness crept, man and horse like a raft of locust. Colors made no difference. Bucket lines had brought down many of the stakewall fires but the artillery placements on that side had been left unsafe. No keg or fuze could be kept so near to live coals. There had been no further orders from the house, and Jacobs began to see that he would be the name in charge of the slaughter to come. Fusiliers retrained the mortars to the weakened side, on his order, and to the small arms he called "At will! At will!"

Three thousand at once, more, coming up the road laid with volunteers. Cannon and mortar opened, drowning out the song. Hundreds bought glory where the ground was shattered and burnt, but most charged clear to the outermost palisades. What was dark now showed green—heavy seas of Graham tartan. All that force did not drive the wind but pull it on their breath, and the ground leapt at their clash.

"All horse defend the cannon!" Jacobs cried. "Repel the Scots! Repel the Scots!"

Brutal, monstrous—men and horses undifferentiated, mouths and eyes and smoke and weapons like the surge of winter swept to rock. Jacobs sallied in, weapon high, to a fierce brawl. His comrades did no less, even as carcass and corpse and victims yet alive teemed beneath the hooves and boots, and the cavalrymen gained no further ground. At the slow ebb animals and Scots were left hung up in the stakes, thrashing out their agonies. With sling the rest began to throw oil, and even as they struggled against the halt more torches were landed in the woodwork, fires kindling fast. Three powder-stores were set alight, and the explosions flung shard and splinter in a reap of head and limb. A long gun came rolling down an embankment, dismounted from its cart, shearing through pales and crushing man and horse. Jacobs leapt from his saddle as his own was bowled out from under. He bobbed along the top of the fighting hordes—hands rising through pot helmet to bear him back—and he came down shoulder-first to reddened mud at the inner side of battle.

The Scots drove, and single riders broke through, to a desperate signal from the horns. Musketeers took most out, and those minding the field turned to shoot inward. A Highland rider burst through the scrum close to Jacobs—bald, burly, and gray-whiskered. He was grinning through swaddles of mud and worse and held a lochaber ax. Not a weapon meant for horseback, but he kept it in a single grip like a mallet for sport. Their eyes met before the charge, and Jacobs searched his chest for the rifle strap, never breaking the stare. The sword had been knocked from his grip. The polearm swung close indeed as Jacobs fired one of his eight chambered shots, chipping off his hat, and the round cracked the smooth head. The horse ran past, and yet another horseman came through, this one a ruddy lad, in a charge for the house. Jacobs levered the next chamber into line and cleared the saddle. Higher ground, he realized—a better vantage could help him take out more. A bloodied and riderless horse trotted close and Jacobs had the bridle.

And he had no sooner swung into the stirrups with a grip on the horn when the mortars' ammo dump went alight.

Nothing—he heard nothing on the titanic clap, not even the rush of his blood. But he saw that the headless horse had pinned him to the broken palisade. Clots were yet raining down and his vision had gone yellowish. Bodies and parts of bodies were all about him, and he could see the Scots and Roundheads standing from the shockwave to renew the fight. Silence was absolute but he heard battle from a distance and once again he saw the day at the bridge. Much the same—on the ground again, helpless as men nearby fought and died. Past and present were a ravel, and he could not say in which he was. He turned from the massacre, struggling against the weight that kept him down. And he saw those Cavaliers once more, the party on horse about Rupert of the Rhine, looking on with shame at the gruesome disport until they could take no more of it. Rupert and his advisor never turned away, one face colder than the other.

A face he had seen then for the first time. Different clothing, same remove—and the selfsame role, but then for the Royalist side.

The uproar came back with Jacobs yet in shock. But fury rose as he realized what he had seen, remembered, and anger brought strength. He hauled himself free and gathered up his rifle where it was hung in the stakes. Looking out he saw all the Scottish cavalry pouring in, and south the tell of more riders to come. And he made toward the heart of the fight—not downward, into that clash of thousands, but to the house, to Sentance.

Who had returned to Makepeace and the horse, there on the terrace. On a shoulder he had brought a pair of saddlebags, fat with provisions. These were secured to the animal. Without a glance, "I'll have pistol on your back."

Makepeace looked out. All northern cavalrymen swarmed the breach, dismounted for the task. To the south a lane of escape stood clear, much as Sentance had predicted. "I'd thank you for all you've done for me," he said, "but I can't recall what any of it was." There was also a messenger's satchel—no documents in it—and to further the ruse he strapped it atop his costume.

Sentance stood off, hand under cloak. "Begone with you."

Makepeace put spurs to the horse. It nickered at rough treatment but leapt into speed. Down the lanes of stakewall he rode, those yet clear of Scots. "Dispatches," the cry went up. "Make way! Small guns hold your fire!" Never recognized for who he was—and none there would ever see him again.

At the rail on the terrace above, that was where Jacobs spied him. Sentance was staring out into the field, scarf down. An easy target, but the captain found all eight rifle chambers spent. Reloading blind was his oldest trick as a rifleman, so his attention never went astray. Nor did that of the man above, whatever it was that he saw on the move out past the fight. Making out the bare face, the look worn, Jacobs felt the anger slip to a disquiet no less awful. Too far to be sure, but he would have put a pretty sum on a smile.

One chamber would suffice it, a lone round, and the hands worked fast. Cylinder clapped to breech and the aim came up, but his target had stepped away.

Jacobs stood from cover. Lieutenant Noakes had been riding back down from the house—arm in a sling, hair burnt on a side clear down to his naked scalp. Once he saw his commander he changed course. Jacobs said, "Take charge," no more, and his eye never quit the hunt. Whatever tricks were in store, Sentance was no less hemmed in there—he had nowhere to go but the river.

To their pride none saw them come. The thirty men who had rafted about the barricade, with driftwood for cover, were among the last of their sort: reivers, all from one bastle house tucked above the borderlands. Rustlers by trade and killers by chance—however lavish killing got—they were supreme horsemen but had been hired out here for stealth. They made good, in truth too easily. The calamity just past the trees made waste of a light step, and fumes were pouring down milky thick. The watch on the planks had been left to a dozen—anxious foot soldiers with signal horns, peering out. River water was draining yet from maud and jack as the last near Roundhead fell from his post, this to a quarrel from a latch bow. Dirks did the rest.

Thirsty chores, and nothing to brag of, but the reivers lost no curiosity on sight of newcomers. Two of them, a man and woman. Not soldiers, nor perhaps even English. With a plashing racket—clumsy, all but drowning—they floundered about the other barricade, south side, where it met the current. Coarse fishes, but game enough.

From behind the stores, grins and hand signs were exchanged. Clear a way, hold the dock: the contract was plain. No riever led but all were of one mind. Who the fools were, that would be a thing to discuss over tall pints once the task was done.

For push Roundhead horse were trained to ride knee to knee, and three thousand made for an overwhelming ram. It had been a quick section of the lowland riders—a few skinned off from the drive—and now they ran hard to the south. A few hundred Scots had given chase, this in spite of standing orders and not a little mad. The backsides of English heretics were too smart a target, and they, too, could read the dust. Swift landing was expected at Morecambe Bay, due north of Lancaster, and therefrom allies would close, the Lowlanders knew. But they had not expected so many. A pale tinge for wet country, but their minds made the sky ahead wholly dark—thunder and gale come up to thwart the rebels.

Instead the Englishmen ahead gave a cheer, louder even than the roll of hooves. Their formation broke in the middle, all horse doubling back. The gap spread, and through it the Lowland riders saw the inspiration.

Thousands, yes—six perhaps—and in that host, cornets bore a field of red.

"Ironsides," the nearest sassenachs were shouting, and to a man. "Ironsides!"


The breach ushered in the Scots—all forward positions overrun, men strewn about the burning pales like tailor's scrap. The bombardment gave out, opening the field, and with a thirsty roar all companies of lowland militia were rejoined to the Highland cavalry. The dead—horse, man, and forms so misused that neither could be said— grew deep in the lanes, too deep to permit horseback. Scots came down off the saddles, and all fighting went to melee. A fiery chaos, horses running free, and such a thunder that the signal almost went unheard. But on horns all Roundheads to positions south or north positions gave up their posts and rushed in for the last desperate clash.

To the rear of the mansion house Jacobs took high ground, at a small split-bough tree. This steadied his aim, and again and again he emptied out his eight chambers. Any Scots yet on horse breaking through for the storehouses and the dock fell from the saddle one by one. The last of eight put the hands to thoughtless work, quicker than a loom, priming the cylinder anew. Jacobs' eye never quit searching the terrain. Never, that was, until the shine of sailcloth drew his attention to the river.

The master on the packet kept well off, past range of musket. He had a crew of four oarsmen, presently sculling against the current to hold them in place. Dour and steady, every man on the boat was looking to the pole behind the dock, as yet bare. The crackle of gunfire went on in the distance, as did the shout, the scream, of countless fighters. "We'll give them time," the master said. "We might rescue some."

Behind the hill the Roundheads yet alive and able fell back from the redoubt. Scots had come in range of the house itself, and the oil slings began to fly. Musketeers posted on the high walk kept up their fire, but they had the best view of the slopes below and the countryside beyond. Nothing showed in their eyes but the aim and the terror, and every man up there knew that he was dead.

Róis had kept the gun out of the water, despite the slip, and she and Vanderas fished each other out. Smoke hung like a valley fog and stank of charcoal. They caught their breath, dripping wet, coughing at the fumes. War came down in bellows but the ground stood clear. Vanderas had been keen on the landing, the signal pole. They saw no one—alive at least. A glance gave up the forms of men on the ground, toppled from the wooden walk, and he went up close to one. Otherwise nobody seemed at home.

"We have to get the colors up," Róis said.

Vanderas had pulled a bolt from the English victim. He inspected it, the shallow fletching, and threw it aside.

"Joaquim," Róis said. "They won't land without the sign."

"Careful, love—we might not be alone." And when he glanced to the pole Vanderas saw the Parliamentary colors skid up the line. "That goes double," he said.

Peering through the haze, Róis saw the packet, the splashes of white aside the gunwales. The prow swung their way, achingly slow.

"At a distance he'd pass for Puritan," Vanderas said. "But for the likes of us two they won't just tie off and cry all aboard, signal or no signal. We'll get the rowboat down—cross whether the packet flies or not. Call it second prize."

She looked only fretful, thinking of the shadow cast over her life, long and fast. It had chased her here as well, no less close than her own would have stood in open sun. "He's up there on the boards somewhere. What should we do? What can we?"

"Distract. I'll draw him out. You take the boathouse and I'll handle the violence."

"Alone, against that?"

"Were they middling my skills could never have brought such grief. You're no good for second in a duel. Better you play the sneak. Let's be off. You pled guilty to the whole damned Roundhead army."

"I'll have no regret of saving you."

"Perhaps we can save each other. Fair's fair."

Their eyes were close in the kiss, and she swept her fingers to his cheek. But as they broke away the happiness was struck from her face. "Joaquim, wait. He—he carries something, so he does. Something I made for him earlier on. Would I'd given him a spoon of treacle instead, the bastard."

Makepeace rode trampled grass for long minutes before the dust cloud grew worrisome. He had expected to see battle sign first—horse on horse—but now it was clear that the southern charge had kept on without resistance. Three Roundhead regiments were no small work, no mere litter, no matter how large the opposing force. He saw a copse of trees and made for it. Once on his feet he pulled the bridle, and with a grunt the horse lay down beside him. He peered out through the underbrush and the shade and listened to the rumble build.

His own were riding back—none lost—and they had company. He knew the ensigns and looked for where the cornets were thickest. On that great tide of horse and soldier, nearly ten thousand strong, and somewhere in the middle, he caught sight of his rival. Tears made a blur of the rest, and Makepeace could not have told relief from sorrow, or shame from pride. He lay there for the better part of an hour after they passed, to a vacuous silence, and the dust continued to sift down through the leaves and the heavy air, to a taste in his mouth.

＊　＊　＊

The country house had gone alight, floor to roof. Flames were licking out in billows through window frame and door, and heat split the wood with a report like shot. Actual gunfire had not let up behind the pike, and the musketeers stationed on the roof had switched vantage to the back. They were trapped by the fire but not yet spent of powder, and they did all they could, firing down on anything in trews or tartan. The redoubt had been completely overrun, save for rearmost positions, and it was here, on Noakes' order, that the remaining foot had fallen back. Narrow approaches on either side of the house kept the Scots in a bottleneck, and the heat of the blaze lent itself to the defense. They pressed on all the same, seeing the end, many in a sweat and some in a blister. No one was left to watch the fields where the fight had begun, and where sign of floods to come would have changed the outlook.

"Keep you long?"

Quiet strides for the dock—padding behind a storehouse with a sly grace—and of course once Vanderas rounded the corner Sentance was standing in the open. In hand was the odachi, and he looked on utterly without surprise. The smoke had grown heavy, and the din of battle had redoubled in the loss of the house.

Róis was somewhere close, in her own stealth, and even for the fury upslope Vanderas hoped to mask the sound. The backsword was up and ready. "I'm short a hand," he said. "You needn't fear a throw—of a knife, say. Where's yours?"

A gloved hand spread the left skirts of the cloak. There, at hip, hung the sheath and dagger. Drawn in no special haste, and a strand grew thinner than a silken strand before it broke. All the blade was slathered, no steel shining through the brackish coat, and the traces burnt the leather of the glove.

"Ooh," Vanderas said, "you flatter me. It can only mean I scare you."

The voice was empty. "Part of a math, is all—one marker on a counter full."

No fluster, save in Vanderas. To goad Sentance off the landing he kept it hid. "Fearless then, eh," he said. "Shameless, too. None see honor in me, and right so, but I do know the meaning of the word."

"Why talk?" Sentance said. "To buy time for a third— if only a moment, and a last fruitless hope." He gave a nod back to the boathouse, many yards behind and dim in the smoke. "And there she is, making her way inside. I never would have let her go."

Eyes ablaze, Vanderas charged. Sentance shifted a foot and swung, rolling through the stroke. The blades rang in the pass, and at once the two turned and had at it again. Attack, feint, parry, misdirect—with odachi alone Sentance drove Vanderas back. For taunt the poisoned knife stayed high in the left grip. A scraping glide put the backsword in check, and Vanderas swung up and out to where Sentance's throat had stood. But the other man had made a turn, and a volt brought Vanderas out of strike. All a retrospect—too fast for thought—and Vanderas felt a change. Anger did not vanish but the mind stood free—gone clear as it had for the boy atop the headland, that first of countless times. Vanderas watched himself move without hindrance, and his movement was the movement of the enemy. Breath came, breath went, and neither man would tire from that intuition. One and the same, yet behind the match of force one advantage hid, even from the man who held it—a motive not his own. Sentance fought for Sentance. Vanderas fought for Róis.

On that the fight began to shift. If anything read in Sentance, it was surprise. The knife came up, but this only split his attack. Each parry flecked venom to the ground like a caustic spittle. Driven back, back, closer to the storehouses.

There fifteen border reivers came into the open.

Vanderas saw them first, and broke his trance. Reading the worry, Sentance made a lunge, and Vanderas tumbled clear. Coming up he caught a glimpse of Róis in the smoke, gone to the boathouse door. He thought to shout, warn her that the ruse was up, but his body thought quicker. Another roll as Sentance's odachi swung down. Tuck and twist, sprung to his feet—Vanderas squared off again.

The reivers had made a semicircle. Behind them canvas atop the storehouses had caught fire. Approach of strangers, and then the duel, had delayed the burn, and half had gone to flank the English. The spectacle of close combat went on without interrupt, even for the audience and the flames, and a kind of admiration.

"Which is wa marra?" said one.

"Neen's one of us," said another. "Mak it nowt."

They closed, fifteen at once. And they grew quite near to the ongoing bout before Sentance and Vanderas both broke off to kill one each.

The storehouse fires drew Jacobs's eye. The bottlenecks stood at the approaches on either side of the house fire. Those Roundheads who remained alive had lost no further ground, and pike and shot held the tide. He saw them silhouetted against the flames, hard at it, a bristle in a kiln. Absorbing work, but wax in the storehouse canvas made for a brighter blaze, almost white, and downslope between two billows Jacobs saw Sentance and Vanderas— and two of fifteen reivers fall.

Reloading without a glance he broke off from the present fight. But here came the other fifteen reivers, and on his cry Roundheads turned to pour in against them.

Sentance had struck with the knife. The border man met the ground with a bluing face. The strangling throes did not go unnoticed by his friends, and they looked to the weapon. The duel went on, more heated than before—

Sentance and Vanderas were both gulping for air, each in hard remise, desperate for their flanks. With hard faces the reivers closed again, this time with focus on the poisoner.

Each show of vulnerability drew a reiver close, and each time he met the knife. Uncanny defense, and in no way hampering the struggle against Vanderas. Another reiver stumbled away, color gone, and another, another. Rage would not let them give him up, only grew, and soon a dozen of the reivers lay dead, eleven livid. A draining effort—Vanderas watched Sentance tire, and knew he would have him.

And he would have, had two of the remaining three reivers not used good sense. From safe range each chose to throw a dagger—one intent on Sentance, the other on Vanderas. In the dodge he had no time to mark the second knife, deflected with a counterstroke from Sentance, to a hard spin. Vanderas's thigh sank the tip, and deep. There, in bone and nerve, it had stuck. A yell, a knee, and the world came up to Vanderas's side, gone hazy in the pain.

The odachi whirled through the remainder. No sound was close but the roar of storehouse fires. Sentance bided time, catching his wind, ever looking to the opponent on the ground. Then he stepped up close.

Vanderas lunged but fell back in agony. There he stood, the man almost undone, watching, nothing in the eyes but attention. The haft of the reiver's knife was slick with blood, and the torment of the pull left a gap. Coming back, Vanderas looked up, to where Sentance held up the knife again, venom shown, awaiting the final eye.

Vanderas found a sneer, a little moisture—enough to spit. "There's your answer," he said. Róis would have got the rowboat in the water, he told himself. Making way to the far bank or to the packet, Róis would be safe, go on. Sabdh had been her name. That could be her only fame again, and where none remembered her, she would remember him. The knife was cocked for a throw. No risk of close murder, no pert remark. Vanderas never looked away, even as the black-clad shoulder burst.

Gunshot—it had torn through, and the crack resounded just after.

Sentance's eyes widened, and his mouth, but he uttered no sound. The arm fell dead, and from the numb hand, the knife. Blood freckled a side of his ashen face. His eyes met Vanderas's once again, as if to share a joke.

The rifle—but one round of eight. Jacobs was yet out of sight, but his field of fire was between the burning stores. Odachi in hand, and with that cover, Sentance made a trot for the boathouse. The step was fast but lurching, the shoulder in a droop.

The boathouse.

Like a clutch lever, knife in living bone. The scream kept Vanderas conscious as he pushed, pulled, pushed, pulled, working it loose. But at last there was give. He yanked the knife from the muscle and the sopping cloth, and blood ran freely. Almost fainting once again, he willed himself upright, and to his feet. With a stoop he took up the backsword, sagged, stood again, tip to earth for a crook. The leg took weight but the flow did not cease. All in sight was a pale shade and swam in and out of focus.

Vanderas turned to the boathouse. A shadow was at the door. Panic made him bolt but no less quickly put him on the ground again.


The rope and the dirk—these made the difference for Róis. The rowboat had been there, raised above the slip on a sheave and double lines, but the winch had not been lowered for many years and hemp was fouled in the groove. A knot, she thought to herself. Another goddam knot. Be damned to knitting. Yet the dirk was not with her, somehow. With fearful clarity, brighter far than anything inside, she saw herself thrust it to the bank, where it yet stood.

So she fought with the tangle, little choice, the sound of warfare muted in the close space. With no less passion she wished for a cutting edge—dirk, shard of glass, a stronger tooth. On boards sprung by weather and neglect the musket lay at her feet. She thought to shoot the line and had a last laugh.

No sooner quit than here he was, on a kick to the door. The plank burst inward and clapped to a wall. Sight of the figure drew a scream, and Róis reeled to a corner. He came on, odachi out. As he neared the winch he made a slash, and the rowboat turned in the drop. The stern bathed the boards in the splash as the prow broke the wood, and her thought was no less a crashing racket as her hand sought in vain for the knitting hooks—one more device left behind.

162

*  *  *

From a dead reiver Vanderas had pulled a belt. This bound the leg, cinched hard and fast above the wound, and the stagger had resumed when he heard the scream. It sped him, and the anguish brought silence. For him there was no gunfire, no spit of flames, no cry of hundreds above the landing—only the ringing aftermath of the scream, that voice he knew. His boots drummed unheard along the timbers, in a thickened smoke, and as he grew close to the door, through a gap in the fumes he saw Sentance just ahead. Looking outward on the river, faced away—the packet had grown close enough to hail.

The backsword came up and Vanderas hastened, mouth dry, face damp and cold. Sentance turned about. Half his face yet wore the stain from the gunshot. But there had not been as much thrown there before.

A nod to the boathouse, and Sentance said, "Will she die alone?"

This Vanderas heard all to well, and the clamor of war came back with it. He stood, he stared, he felt the pull. And he watched himself turn and make quick for the door, the chase given up, even as the packet came to range of the pier. Sentance leapt with a running start, sword out high, coming down on the master of the boat, who had only seen a lone wounded man on the river pier, a man in need of aid.

\* \* \*

Unreal, too real, the dim interior of that shed and the moment that came. Before his eyes were ready for the dark he heard her breath, harsh and fast, and took hope. The capsized rowboat hid the sight of her until he skirted the broken boards. And sight of her was hidden yet even in the open. His mind refused it. Slumped against a wall, both hands to her neck, clutching hard. Her eyes were wild, more white shown than green. Below that clutch the hands were dark and slick, and everything below the hands—every scrap of clothes, inch of bare skin. A spatter tracked down the boards like dew, and the gaps in the wood on the floor where she sat let it drain.

The backsword was in his hand, and then not. He heard no clatter as he rushed up to her, dropping to his knees with a skid. Blood—undeniable blood—it ran fast between her fingers, yet the wound was not so deep that she had lost it instantly. Sentance had started her like an hourglass. Thereby he had bought time for the escape. Vanderas had no thought of that, not yet. They shared the panic, and the words were a ravel.

"Let me help you—"

"Don't, don't touch my hands—"

"I'll bring a surgeon, love, press a cloth against—"

"It's—oh Mary, Mary forgive—"

"You'll be all right, you'll—"

"I'm frightened, Joaquim love, oh so frightened, all I've done, it's unconfessed—listen, listen now—take my confession to a priest, do you hear—take me to a priest with my confession, once I'm—oh Mary—these, these English won't even bury me, just throw me in the river or leave me to rot—"

His face was close to hers, and the sob overtook him. Hands went to her, away again, stained with her life, afraid to touch.

Her eyes were fluttering and narrow, and her breath grew calm, her voice quiet. "Take my confession—listen— remember all I say, all I've done, remember—"

To catch the whisper, grown faint, he set his ear close to her mouth. Her lips brushed at him as they parted, almost a kiss, and her hands fell from the neck. His own shot up, grasping at the wound, almost to a strangle.

"Tell me, love," he managed, in a whisper of his own. He listened close again. "Tell me what to say—what to do."

The breath left her all at once—a sigh, deep but untroubled, that spoke into his ear. For the repulsion, refusal again, a gust might have thrown him back, and his shoulders struck the wreck of the boat. There was nothing in his senses but Róis where she lay—Róis gone still, terribly still, as inert as the timbers that held her upright. Blood was all over him from the last touch, and it mingled with his own. Her struggles had bared an ankle, close to his reach. There he felt the last of her warmth.

The rattle was yet in his ear, a sound the man born there would hear for the remainder of his life. No passage of time, no thought—sight of her like that dug raw and bitter, all of him hollowed out. His fingers lost the hold on her foot, and to prop him up, to keep her there in his sight, he dragged the hand back to himself, a deadweight on the wrist. With a faintest tap it brushed the unseen hilt and nudged the backsword on the floor—a scrape that was hardly any noise at all.

The shift was instant, or shift at all. Grief was rage, rage grief, and it burnt him shut. Soon the boathouse door flew from its hinges—a mindless kick, rabid strength—and Vanderas ran out to the end of the dock. The packet had come about in a desperate row and the sail dragged against the wind. Already it was twenty yards off. There stood Sentance, looking back to his enemy, with the odachi and a pistol drawn, looming over the crew of rowers. The master lay in a slump on the transom, and his mortal wound had painted the stern and left a cloud in the wake. Sentance looked to the sail fouling on the breeze and slashed at the sheet. Down came the sailcloth, and his captives shied at the stroke, rowing yet harder.

Vanderas looked about. There was no thought but slow murder—torment of the man so near and of any who stood in the way. Through the smoke he spotted a cannon above the southernmost barricades, upright yet.

A high vantage, and an aim downriver. The position was overrun by Scots, well behind the Roundhead line of pike. Not many were left, a few hundred against thousands, and Jacobs fought among them, too engrossed in the last reivers and a northern sea to reload his gun. It was sword and knife against the reivers and any who forced a way through—sword and knife hewn to with a fierce speed. All men were exhausted, the massacre coming on in fits and starts and a gasp of breath.

No thought, no flinch, only a rush for the cannon. There was no sense of pain, nor of the leg itself. No limp, no slowing, even as the wound resumed to bleed and the shock on injured bone made the face go pale. Vanderas flew between the roaring storehouses, and sparks lit into his hair and eyes. Go and do—nothing else, no human mind—and bright fire closed behind him.

Sentance did not miss the hurry from the boat. He looked to what had drawn the interest. An oarsmen felt a pistol at the back of his head.

"Hasten us."

The reivers made slow work through the flank of the defense, one Roundhead butchered out at a time. Jacobs scarcely kept the sword raised, and the patch had come off his eye. The gaping hole had a stare all its own, a countenance half death. Behind pike and Scots there was a tremendous crash as fire staved in the roof of the mansion house. The musketeers up top fell in or leapt forward, three stories onto rough ground, and the high gunfire stopped.

Jacobs foundered, took a knee, and thought to raise a parry without life in the sword arm. But a reiver saw the chance—made a target of that skullish gape—and brought a dirk high in a fist.

A fist chipped off, along with the dirk. Vanderas had thrown himself in, and the abandonment was like nothing any man could see in nightmares. Knee and elbow, head and neck, reivers fell crippled or dead at once. Jacobs looked up in time to glimpse the face, and what he saw was madness—the selfsame face he had witnessed long before. Grisly, but the Roundheads cheered. Their flank made safe and with a glimmer of hope, the defense was recruited.

Vanderas ran on without pause—between two pikemen, much to their astonishment. All the other side was a breathy leering wall of Scots, and Vanderas snapped and snarled against them like something on a chain. The pikemen saw the fear in the enemy—parting for the backsword and more for the lunatic—and they found the strength to push.

And so he fought, maimed, killed without heart, all the way to the gun as Scots were beaten back. He never heard the trumpets of the Ironsides, pouring in at last, or the joy of the Roundhead survivors, loud and hearty. Call went up among the Scots to form a line, to confusion. Vanderas had reached the cannon, and the gruesome path he had laid to it was trod over by the English rushing at the Scots.

Dead fusiliers were at the barrel and the wheels. One yet held a swab, and near to another was a pail of lit match. Vanderas looked down the bore and saw the cartridge—loaded, never fired. With his last energies he pushed against the gun, adjusting the aim to the river. Six hundred yards out the packet was stirring up a foam. He slipped, turned, put a back into it, bellowing at the strain. The injured leg gave out, and the boot yet planted scraped a furrow with the heel. But at last the cannon shifted.

Roundheads were pouring past, giving chase, and Jacobs had found the will to get up and follow. As he stumbled past the gun position he saw Vanderas hauling himself up the wheel spokes, a cord of match in hand, legs dead. The match found the touch-hole, and the bore leapt beneath, throwing Vanderas among the slain.

Jacobs glanced out to the river, and there saw the target. A plume of water shot up—a hundred yards shy. With a frown he went on, reloading the rifle gun with well-trained hands, and joined in the final fight. Nine thousand English cavalry had swept across the vale and up to the redoubt, and it was a lucky Scot indeed who managed to escape. The battle went on, and by arms alone Vanderas hauled himself upright again, looking out on the boat—untouched and much farther out. A crate of artillery was yet ready, near the cannon, and in the pail the match smoldered on. But his leg would not come back, and he felt the cold shock in it spread through him. Shivering, gritting his teeth, he squirmed toward his backsword where it had fallen on the clap. Near he saw a musket, perhaps with a shot, but fatigue and blood loss had caught up. His hand would not close on the hilt, or on the gun, and chest and cheek struck the earth. From that groveling perch above the river, his face turned for last sight of the boat, grown small, gone. Sentance had known how to buy the time, and there lay the fault. Too used up to shut the eyes, to look away, and too full of sorrow even to weep.

\*　\*　\*

In time he watched his ghost venture back downhill. The fallen were more like a rubble than a crowd of human beings, so great was the number, so awful the harm. Some vault had come crashing down to earth. His feet found a way among them, stepping for dirt in snares and ruts among the limbs, and he did so with a slow method and nothing like a present mind. The ground ran and sopped with what it stank of, what stained every piece of cloth and skin within sight. He had little of the stuff left himself and even that moderate pace left him pale and mottled. The pulse and breath raced behind the sweat. But none of those were him. The arms were cold below the elbow, and the feet, and there was only one purpose in the thoughts.

In the distance Roundheads had been celebrating for a time, met up with their cousins, their saviors, the last Scots driven off. Each storehouse was a smoldering pit, and in near silence embers spat and coughed among the blackened frames. When Vanderas came out of the boathouse she had been wrapped in a sheet—the Parliamentary ensign, struck from the pole. He took her past the ashes to a cart that had been left untouched. Feed straw had been spread out from a broken bale. How he managed to carry her in that state would be no less sure than the memory. Gently he lay her in the bed and, with less expression on his face than she wore on hers, set a hand to her brow.

A noise drew his attention—the hapless High Anglican. He had a team of volunteers behind him, looking for the wounded and giving rites to anything dead. He never saw Vanderas until the shadow crept up his surplice, and he raised eyes to a dark-haired man as white as wax, in rags drying to a crust. One arm led him, and the other held the backsword. Once the priest was at the cart the grip on his forearm gave up. No others were close, but the volunteers looked on from their chores with frightful glances. The priest glanced between the harrowed man and the slain woman, and he turned a flap of the Parliamentary ensign from her face.

"Absolve her," Vanderas said in English.

"She's a papist, is she not? An Irish girl?"

"Absolve her."

"What are her sins? Can either of us say?"

The edge of the backsword was at the priest's neck—a light press that stung without a cut. But the arm was trembling, to a reckless shave. "Absolve her," Vanderas said again, and his voice had no more force.

The Roman Catholic rite was not far from the High Anglican, though words and language differed. Nervously, the priest did his best. "Dominus noster Jesus Christus te absolvat; et ego auctoritate ispius te absolvo ab omni vinculo suspensionis et interdicti in quantum possum et tu indiges." With the sign of the cross, "Deinde, ego te absolvo a peccatis tuis in nomine Patris, et Filii, et Spiritus Sancti. Amen."

The weapon came off and was resheathed, with a trembling rattle. Vanderas reached to the cloth and covered up the face once more. The hand lay on the cheek—white fingers, bluing nails.

"Son," the priest said, with some distance. "It isn't a matter for rhyme and rote. With the Lord there are no mere formalities, not where damnation is concerned."

The eyes were glassy as they came up—no threat, hardly wakeful—but the priest flinched back all the same. The stare broke, and Vanderas looked to a havoc that spread as far as any eye could see—and that spread yet, soaking deep into the English mud, and seeping into the river course.

His voice was no more than a rustle of the throat. "Then I'll see her again." With that he let himself collapse, all his wretched part played out.

Woodlands kept him out of sight, biding two days' aimless trot, waiting for a plan to present itself. The garb of an army messenger was yet on him, dirty and knee and elbow. He kept clear of travelers on the road, be they peasant, townsman, or comrades at arms. The horse would stop for graze and for water at any stream or pond, and he would dismount and wait for his turn upon its time again.

Past sadness, past shame—a dull being without taste nor appetite. Still, when the horse put a snout to weeds on that second afternoon, he took down a saddlebag and a hunt flask. These he took beneath a tree. Neither had been touched until then. By wits alone he knew he was hungry, and more so had a thirst. The stores gave up hard cheese and flatbread, and dutifully he ate a quarter share of each. To no particular sight, he stared out as he pulled the stopper from the flask, and no muses came to visit. Crumb was yet in his teeth, and as took a drink—a small beer—he made note, even through the swallow, of the strong taste, the first since fleeing from his name.

Flask yet in hand, he sat bolt upright. He recalled what she had said the day before the rout, even in her living voice. "Like pepper and honey it's told. Not bitter of itself, but plain and startling." With something near a laugh he recalled the rest. "A wet demise, and horrible, like drowning abed."

The final measure of his defeat. He stood up and went back to the horse. Taking but a single item he left it to its business. And once he had gone to a seat deeper in the woods, far deeper, there to pass a moment—a rake of sun through branch and leaf, the slow brushes of wind, the rumor of birds—the horse made no story of the shot. It only bent an ear, heard no more, and went back to forage.

On a cot, all wounds sewn, dressed, and cauterized, Vanderas came to. A young man, one of the Ironsides' servant lads, had been posted to keep watch. On sight of open eyes, he dashed from the tent. Vanderas heard him cry, "Colonel! Colonel Jacobs, sir!" He glanced about. The scene was familiar—twice he had thought himself gone, only to return, and only once did he regret it straight away. On a table beside him were his gear and weaponry, and a change of clothes.

In came Jacobs. He took a chair to wait. Vanderas did not move or look, but at last he spoke. "Have that eye now?"

Jacobs said nothing.

"What have you done with her?"

"Shall I take you?"

The dressing went slow, and not just for the bind of suture and bandage. All his body sang with injury. The backsword in its scabbard served well for a walking stick, or well enough. But at last Jacobs led him out to a horse and gig. The look of the camp near the site of battle told him that days had passed, three at least. In turn the gig bore them to a stand of trees above the river. Even before he slid down from the bench, Vanderas saw the unmarked patch of dirt. Two yards long, one deep. Little feeling, or little he could name aside from purpose.

"The men resented it," Jacobs said. "Or her part, I should say. But it was done for your sake. In the end you saved more lives—the last of my fellow soldiers and likely mine as well. With you it's an accident. Recurrent, but a happy one of late."

Vanderas stood reckoning the dirt. Kneeling down slow, and brushed up a handful, sifting through it with thumb to feel the texture. "The Scots stood between me and the gun, Jacobs," he said. "Had the English done the same, so would I."

"That's not what happened. You've been reprieved, and I've been promoted."

174

"A purse. Please."

Jacobs puzzled at it, demand for pay. But he did not stint for a sack of coins. What happened on the toss puzzled him more: at arms' length Vanderas poured the coins out and kept the velvet sack. "Shall we—would you like to put up a stone?"

Back to Jacobs, Vanderas worked the soil, but the colonel knew well enough what he was doing in that crouch. "Let none disturb her," Vanderas said. "Leave her to her peace. Sadbh was her name. You never knew it, but I did." With a purse newly full he stood. The furrows where he had scraped up the grave dirt had been patted smooth. The drawstring took a pull, cinched tight, before he stashed the keepsake in his clothes. "By now he's reached the sea."

"Makepeace?"

"The other. Makepeace is nothing."

"The general's nowhere to be found. But in the thick some saw a messenger ride out. There had never been an order. It's plain enough. The new head of the Northern Association held a court martial in absentia. There's a warrant on him, signed by Oliver Cromwell himself."

He looked Jacobs in the eye. The gaze was not haunted or hurt or diminished in any way. Instead, the colonel saw the old madness, and more—a madness grown sure. "Makepeace is nothing," Vanderas said again. "He took advice. Justice or none, he took it to the very end."

On the return to camp evening had fallen. The priest and several deacons were yet at work preparing the dead, and the man in charge spared a nervous eye. The country folk had turned out of course—even more of them than before, to boil the water and dig the holes. Figures sewn into sheets were arrayed no less neatly than they had stood at inspection during their careers. On they sprawled, to acres, thousands of reverent dead. The Scots were burnt, however, in careless pyres out on the field that stank of roast.

Vanderas made no study of the change. He had told Jacobs what he would need, and soon enough a horse and outfit was brought to his disposal. He sorted through the gear and strapped it on, with fingers and joints grown less stiff. The colonel came up with his eight-shot snaphaunce in hand, retrieved quickly from his bivouac.

"You'd ride at night in a brigand's country?"

No answer, but Vanderas sensed the offering before he looked. No move to take it, not at first, only a flat stare.

"We weren't the only ones at the bridge," Jacobs said. "He was, too, there behind Rupert. I only caught a glimpse, and it came back to me. Some would look on this disaster and think he was a Royal spy. But I see it better than that. And I understand. You're a disloyal man, Vanderas—a killer for hire. But there is someone worse than you, far worse. I pray this might help us be rid of him someday."

"I can't shoot a rifle, Jacobs."

"Learn then. As I did. The man you'd chase knows how."

There was no show of thanks as Vanderas took the gift. Stock and barrel were lashed to the horse behind the cantle—no ceremony, no real care.

"I won't call you friend," Jacobs said. "But I can grieve for you—even look on you and your lot with pity." Vanderas did not seem to listen. He swung himself onto the horse, gasping at the pain, and Jacobs went on. "War ends. For most men it's a brief trade. It ends, and they retire to hearth and home. Back in London I have a wife, a wife and child, and when this is done I'll have a use for myself, for their sake. But you—such brilliance with a weapon, and such tales. Done of strife, peace be made, it's all for nothing. You have nowhere to go. I've never met a man who had so little."

"I have an enemy," Vanderas said, and a snap of reins took him into the dusk.

End